# MANDIE®
## AND THE
## WASHINGTON NIGHTMARE

# *Mandie® Mysteries*

1. *Mandie and the Secret Tunnel*
2. *Mandie and the Cherokee Legend*
3. *Mandie and the Ghost Bandits*
4. *Mandie and the Forbidden Attic*
5. *Mandie and the Trunk's Secret*
6. *Mandie and the Medicine Man*
7. *Mandie and the Charleston Phantom*
8. *Mandie and the Abandoned Mine*
9. *Mandie and the Hidden Treasure*
10. *Mandie and the Mysterious Bells*
11. *Mandie and the Holiday Surprise*
12. *Mandie and the Washington Nightmare*
13. *Mandie and the Midnight Journey*
14. *Mandie and the Shipboard Mystery*
15. *Mandie and the Foreign Spies*
16. *Mandie and the Silent Catacombs*
17. *Mandie and the Singing Chalet*
18. *Mandie and the Jumping Juniper*
19. *Mandie and the Mysterious Fisherman*
20. *Mandie and the Windmill's Message*
21. *Mandie and the Fiery Rescue*
22. *Mandie and the Angel's Secret*
23. *Mandie and the Dangerous Imposters*
24. *Mandie and the Invisible Troublemaker*
25. *Mandie and Her Missing Kin*
26. *Mandie and the Schoolhouse's Secret*
27. *Mandie and the Courtroom Battle*
28. *Mandie and Jonathan's Predicament*
29. *Mandie and the Unwanted Gift*
30. *Mandie and the Long Good-bye*
31. *Mandie and the Buried Stranger*
32. *Mandie and the Seaside Rendezvous*
33. *Mandie and the Dark Alley*
34. *Mandie and the Tornado!*
35. *Mandie and the Quilt Mystery*
36. *Mandie and the New York Secret*
37. *Mandie and the Night Thief*

---

- *Mandie Datebook* · *Mandie Diary*
- *Mandie and Joe's Christmas Surprise*
- *Mandie and Mollie: The Angel's Visit*
- *Mandie's Cookbook*

03B

# MANDIE® AND THE WASHINGTON NIGHTMARE

Lois Gladys Leppard

BETHANY HOUSE PUBLISHERS
MINNEAPOLIS, MINNESOTA 55438

*Mandie and the Washington Nightmare*
Copyright © 1989
Lois Gladys Leppard

MANDIE® is a registered trademark of
Lois Gladys Leppard

Library of Congress Catalog Card Number
88–63464

ISBN 1–55661–065–3

Cover illustration by Chris Wold Dyrud

All rights reserved.
No part of this publication may be reproduced, stored in a retrieval system, or transmitted in any form or by any means—electronic, mechanical, photocopying, recording, or otherwise—without the prior written permission of the publisher and copyright owners.

Published by Bethany House Publishers
11400 Hampshire Avenue South
Bloomington, Minnesota 55438
www.bethanyhouse.com

Bethany House Publishers is a Division of
Baker Book House Company, Grand Rapids, Michigan.

Printed in the United States of America

For Robert H. McLane,
My Greenville High drama teacher, Greenville Little Theatre director, and valued friend, who taught me dialogue and characterization, and to whom I owe so much.

*About the Author*

LOIS GLADYS LEPPARD worked in Federal Intelligence for thirteen years in various countries around the world. She now makes her home in South Carolina.

The stories of her mother's childhood as an orphan in western North Carolina are the basis for many of the incidents incoporated in this series.

Visit her Web site: www.Mandie.com

# *Contents*

"A man's pride shall bring him low;
but honor shall uphold the humble in spirit"
(Proverbs 29:23).

## Chapter 1 / Where Is Miss Hope?

Pushing open the door, Mandie Shaw stepped into her room at the Misses Heathwoods' School for Girls.

Celia, her roommate, instantly jumped up. "Mandie, I'm so glad you're back! Are you going to Washington, D.C.?" she asked her friend eagerly. "Are you going?"

Mandie looked puzzled. "How did you get back to school before I did?" she asked. Removing her winter coat, she plopped down on the rug in front of the warm fire in the fireplace. "When you left our house in Franklin, you and your mother were going to visit relatives."

Celia sat down beside her. "We cut the visits short so I wouldn't have to rush to get back to school," she explained. "Besides, I was ready to come back after that long Christmas vacation. And I couldn't wait to hear whether you found a way to accept President McKinley's invitation to attend his second inauguration." She sat forward, tossing back her long auburn curls. "Did you, Mandie? Are you going?"

Mandie smiled, but she was sure Celia could see the sadness in her blue eyes. "You know how much I want to go, but . . ." She paused, and there was a catch in her voice as she continued. "I haven't found anyone to go with me yet. And it doesn't look like I will."

"Oh, Mandie!" Celia heaved a big sigh. "It isn't every day that the President of the United States invites a twelve-year-old girl to visit him," she said. "That makes you special. We've just got to figure out a way."

"Well, you know my mother can't go with me because the baby is due soon, and Uncle John wouldn't let her stay alone at home then, either."

"Your grandmother can't get out of her trip to Europe with her friends?"

Mandie shook her head. "No. Their plans have been made for a long time. And I don't know anyone else to ask." Standing up, she walked over to the window seat and sat down, staring outside at the cold, bare trees.

Celia followed. "Mandie, maybe Miss Hope could go with you," she suggested.

"Oh, no, Celia. She has to stay here and help Miss Prudence run the school." Mandie looked pleadingly at her friend. "Celia, would you please keep this invitation a secret until I am positively, absolutely sure whether I'm going or not? I'd rather no one here at the school knew about it right now."

"Of course," Celia replied. "I won't tell a single soul until you say it's all right." Her green eyes twinkled. "But I would like everybody to know that I was at your house when the President's messenger brought you the message—that is, after you tell me I can."

Mandie smiled. "I'll let you spread the word as soon as I know something definite."

"Just imagine," Celia said, staring out the window. "This all came about because the President heard about the hospital you're having built for the Cherokees with the gold you and Joe and Sallie found."

"Uncle Ned is supposed to let me know how the hospital is coming along before I go to see President McKinley. That is, *if* I go to see the President," Mandie finished, her voice betraying the hopelessness.

There was a knock on the door, and Celia hurried to open it.

Uncle Cal, the old Negro caretaker for the school, stepped into the room carrying Mandie's luggage. "We sho' glad to see y'all back," he said, placing the bags in the corner next to the big bureau. "Gits kinda lonesome 'round heah without y'all to liven things up now and den." As he straightened, he turned and flashed a mischievous grin at his wife, Aunt Phoebe, who entered the room behind him.

Aunt Phoebe's black face shone. "Yeh, now things'll start lookin' up," she teased.

Mandie jumped up to hug the old woman. "Oh, Aunt Phoebe, I've missed you and Uncle Cal."

Aunt Phoebe laughed. "We'se glad you's back, Missy," she said. Then looking around the room, she added, "Ain't seed no mouses 'round heah either since y'all been gone home."

Mandie and Celia looked at each other and shivered. The last time they had been away on a holiday, they had come back to find April Snow putting a mouse in the chifferobe where they hung their clothes.

Mandie's eyes narrowed. "Has April Snow been in our room?" she asked.

Aunt Phoebe took Mandie's dresses out of the luggage Uncle Cal brought and began hanging them in the chifferobe. "Don't y'all know? Dat big Yankee girl she done went home fo' Christmas, too. Her ma come aftuh her at de last minute, and she ain't come back yet, neither," she explained.

"Is she coming back here to school?" Celia asked.

"Far as I knows she is," the old woman replied, reaching to put Mandie's hatbox on top of the chifferobe next to Celia's. "I heerd her ma tell Miss Hope dat she gwine t' be late gittin' back—maybe next Monday—'cause dey's gwine t' Noo Yawk City fo' Christmas."

"New York City?" Mandie said in surprise. "That's an awfully long trip."

"Oh, Mandie, you've never been to New York," Celia chided.

"No, but remember Dr. Plumbley, who helped us find the hidden treasure from that map we found? He was from New York City," Mandie answered. "And he talked to us about how far away it is. Besides, you can look on the map in our geography book. It's almost all the way to the top of the United States."

Uncle Cal headed for the hall. "I'se gotta git mo' luggage fo' de other young ladies," he said.

Aunt Phoebe followed. "I bettuh git back downstairs, too," she said. "I'se got things to do. It be 'bout eatin' time."

"Aunt Phoebe." Mandie stopped her. "Will you please let us know when April Snow does come back to school so we can watch out for her?"

"I sho' will, Missy. Now y'all be gittin' ready to eat while I goes and gits it on de table," the old black woman said, disappearing down the hallway.

Celia closed the door. "Did you bring Snowball back, just in case that mouse shows up?" she asked.

"He's at Grandmother's," Mandie replied. "Ben met us at the depot with Grandmother's rig then went by the

Mannings' and got Hilda. He dropped Grandmother and Hilda off at Grandmother's house—along with Snowball—then brought me back to school here."

Celia turned to the mirror on the bureau and brushed a few strands of hair into place. "I'm glad your grandmother lives here in Asheville," she said with a little laugh. "She comes in handy sometimes."

Mandie smoothed her skirt in front of the full-length mirror on a stand in the corner. "I don't think I'll change clothes," she decided. "I'll just keep these on that I wore on the train."

Celia eyed the dark blue traveling suit Mandie was wearing. "I've already changed mine," she said. "I didn't feel comfortable in my suit." She twirled around, fluffing out the long full skirt of the green wool dress she wore.

"Oh, I suppose I will, too," Mandie said with a sigh. "Aunt Phoebe has already hung up my dresses for me." Quickly opening the chifferobe and taking down a blue wool dress, she unbuttoned the traveling suit, stepped out of the skirt, and threw off the jacket and blouse. Then she put on the blue dress and hastily began buttoning it.

Celia smiled her approval. "Now, don't you feel better?"

Mandie shook out her skirt. "I sure do," she replied. Then grabbing the clothes she had just taken off, she started to hang them up when the big bell in the back yard of the school began ringing for the evening meal.

Mandie tossed the clothes in a heap on the big chair nearby. "I'll hang them up when I come back after supper," she said, rushing to the door. "Let's go. We don't want to be late on our first day back."

Celia followed her down the stairs from their third-floor room. "Don't forget our New Year's resolutions for

1901," she reminded Mandie. "We said we'd be on time for everything this year."

"Yes, I've decided to make this year better than last year," Mandie called back over her shoulder.

In the hallway outside the dining room the students waited in line until Aunt Phoebe opened the French doors. Mandie and Celia went in with the other students and stood next to each other behind their assigned chairs until Miss Prudence took her place at the head of the table. Picking up the little silver bell by her plate, the headmistress shook it, and the girls quietly listened.

"Welcome back, young ladies," the short, thin woman greeted them. "I hope you all had a nice Christmas and that you have resolved to study harder this year. As you all know, our mid-year examinations will be held on Thursday and Friday of this week. Until they are completed, no one will be permitted to leave the school for any reason whatsoever. All free time will be spent in reviewing for these tests. Is that clear?"

"Yes, Miss Prudence," the girls replied in chorus.

Miss Prudence looked around the table, and her eyes stopped at April Snow's empty place. "I believe you are all present now except for April Snow," she said. "She has special permission to be late in returning to school. She will take her examinations when she returns."

Miss Prudence hurriedly continued on, raising her voice slightly. "And in case any of the rest of you are thinking about being late for examinations, there is a late fee charged if they are not taken on time." She looked around the table with a stern expression. "Are there any questions?"

After a moment's silence, Mandie spoke up. "Miss Prudence, would you please tell us how April got to act in the play we went to see at Mr. Chadwick's School before Christmas?"

Celia caught her breath in alarm. Even though Miss Prudence asked for questions, the girls simply did not ask her anything. If they had a question, they always went to Miss Hope, Miss Prudence's sister. She was exactly the opposite of the strict headmistress.

Miss Prudence straightened her shoulders and looked directly at Mandie. "That incident is school business," she answered sternly. "And I need not explain anything to you about it. However, I will divulge some of what happened as a lesson to you all."

She paused to look around the table and then continued. "While April Snow was conversing with some of the boys at Mr. Chadwick's School before the dinner, she found that the boy who was supposed to do the part of Mary did not want to do a woman's role. So just before the play began, April slipped backstage and persuaded him to give her a copy of his lines. That's all there is to it," she finished with finality.

Miss Prudence glanced around the room. "However, since April did not have permission to become involved in that way, I want you all to know that she has been punished," the headmistress told them. "And let this be a warning to you that we will not condone any such behavior from any student in this school again. Does that satisfy your curiosity, Amanda?"

Mandie's face flushed red in embarrassment. "Yes, ma'am," she answered meekly.

"Then let's hear no more about it from any of you," Miss Prudence demanded. She changed the subject. "Now, I had informed you before Christmas that we were having electric wires and one of those new furnaces installed. However, the workmen are behind schedule, and it may be awhile before they can install ours. Now . . ." She paused as Miss Hope came rushing into the room and hurried to her sister's side.

"Why, what's wrong, sister?" Miss Prudence asked.

As Miss Hope gestured frantically and whispered something into Miss Prudence's ear, the girls watched and tried to listen.

Miss Prudence quickly shook her little silver bell. "Amanda, you return thanks," she said loudly. "I'll be right back."

The girls watched curiously as Miss Prudence hurried out of the room with Miss Hope, and soon they were buzzing with questions.

Mandie tapped lightly on her glass with her fork. "Girls," she said, trying to get their attention, "let's return thanks."

The room became silent as every head bowed.

Mandie nervously grabbed Celia's hand and said, "We thank Thee, dear God, for the wonderful food we are about to partake of and all the many blessings you have bestowed upon us. Please don't let it be anything bad that called Miss Prudence out of the room. Thank you, dear Lord. Amen."

The girls looked up at Mandie, pulled out their chairs and sat down. Even though the headmistress was not present, the girls passed the food in an orderly manner and kept silent except for a faint whisper here and there.

Mandie looked at Celia as she passed the biscuits. "Must be something awfully important," she whispered.

"Right," Celia whispered back. "Let's hurry and eat so we can find out what happened."

All the girls seemed to have the same idea. Quickly

finishing their meal, they were waiting to be dismissed from the table when Miss Prudence hurried back into the room and sat down. She looked as though she had something important on her mind. When she saw that all the girls were finished eating, she said, "You may all be dismissed now. But go straight to your rooms. No socializing. Only studying is permitted tonight. And please make sure that you *do* study. Good night."

The girls told each other good night as they hurriedly left the table. Mandie and Celia were the first ones out of the dining room, but they slowed down in the hallway to talk.

"What do you suppose happened?" Celia asked her friend as they watched the others head for their rooms.

"Whatever it was, it upset Miss Prudence," Mandie replied. "She looked worried."

"We could go through the kitchen and see if Aunt Phoebe knows what happened," Celia suggested.

"Yes," Mandie agreed. She turned toward the kitchen door and then stopped. "No, remember our New Year's resolutions? Besides, we might get caught."

"You're right," Celia replied as the last of the girls filed past them. "Let's just go to our room."

As the two headed upstairs, they met a group of girls coming down for the second sitting of supper, which Miss Hope usually presided over.

Mandie stopped Celia on the stairs. "I have a feeling that Miss Hope will not be here for the second sitting," she said.

"Why?" Celia asked.

"Well, we haven't seen her since she came in to talk to Miss Prudence, and she seemed to be all flustered or something," Mandie explained. "Let's stand right here until everyone goes into the dining room, and then let's peek in the door and see."

"Mandie, we'll get into trouble if we're caught," Celia warned.

"Nobody will see us if we're careful," Mandie told her.

Celia heaved a big sigh but stayed with Mandie on the stairs, waiting until the other group of girls had entered the dining room. Then they softly crept back down the stairs and tiptoed over to the French doors.

Sure enough, there was Miss Prudence still sitting at the head of the table as the other girls took their seats.

Celia tugged at Mandie's arm, and the two headed back to the foot of the stairs. They stopped.

"You see," Mandie whispered, "something important must have happened. Miss Hope is not here to eat supper."

"Come on, Mandie," Celia urged, running up the stairs.

Mandie quickly followed her friend all the way up the stairs to their room on the third floor.

Finding their books, the two girls sat down on the rug in front of the blazing fire in the fireplace.

Mandie opened her geography book and looked at the fire curiously. "Somebody has built up our fire," she said. "It wasn't going that strong when we went downstairs."

"Probably Aunt Phoebe or Uncle Cal," Celia replied.

Mandie shook her head. "Aunt Phoebe is supposed to be in the kitchen during meals, and I'm pretty sure Uncle Cal helps her down there," she said.

Celia picked up one of her books. "Oh, well. It feels good," she remarked.

Mandie couldn't keep her mind on studying. "I sure

made a mistake asking Miss Prudence about April getting into that play, didn't I?"

"I'll say you did," Celia agreed. "I wouldn't have had the nerve to ask Miss Prudence a question."

"I don't know why I did it. I guess I just wasn't thinking," Mandie mused.

"Mandie, don't you think we are always running into an awful lot of mysteries?" Celia asked.

Mandie turned to her friend and smiled. "No," she replied. "Mysteries are always running into us."

## Chapter 2 / What's Going On?

The next morning Mandie and Celia got dressed earlier than usual and wandered into the parlor to wait for breakfast. Even though some of the other girls were early risers, too, everyone seemed to congregate in the hallways before meals.

Although the students seldom went into the parlor that time of day, a fire blazed in the huge fireplace. Fires were built in all the rooms of the house in cold weather whether the rooms were used or not. Miss Prudence liked the luxury of a warm house.

Mandie warmed herself in front of the fire. "In a way I'll be glad when we get that new furnace here," she told Celia. "It'll be nice to have constant heat like they have in Edwards' Dry Goods Store downtown. But I will miss the pretty fires crackling and jumping in the fireplaces." She rubbed her hands together in the warmth of the flames.

Celia bent over beside her to enjoy the heat. "I know what you mean. An open fireplace is so romantic and beautiful, and I love the smell of wood burning."

"Why, Celia," Mandie said, straightening to look at her friend with new appreciation. "I do believe you are getting

to be poetic. Why don't you write a poem about the fireplace?"

Celia looked up. "Me, write a poem? Oh, Mandie, you're teasing," she replied.

"No, I'm serious, Celia. You ought to try it. I know! Do it for extra credit in English class."

"Well, if I'm going to write a poem," Celia told her, "then I think you ought to write a story about some of the mysteries we've solved. Maybe you could get extra credit for that."

"Oh, I don't know," Mandie said doubtfully. "I'm not sure I'd want everyone to know all the details of some of our adventures."

"If I write a poem, you can be sure it won't be about anything that's true," Celia remarked. Seeing the newspaper lying on a table nearby, she added, "But, Mandie, you could probably write stories for the newspaper."

Following her friend's glance, Mandie walked over and picked up the newspaper, scanning its pages. "I don't think the newspaper prints the kind of stories I'd write." Suddenly she gasped and held the newspaper out to Celia. "Oh, no. Look!" she cried. "It says here that President McKinley is ill with a cold, and his doctor has advised him to stay in his room for three or four days. Celia, the President is sick!"

Celia quickly skimmed the article. "But, Mandie, he only has a cold," she said. "Everybody has a cold now and then."

"But what if he gets too ill to be inaugurated?" Mandie worried.

"I would imagine that he's so eager to get inaugurated again that he'll make it, cold or no cold," Celia assured her.

"Yes, I suppose so," Mandie agreed.

The bell in the backyard rang for breakfast, and the two girls quickly joined the line to the dining room.

Miss Prudence herself opened the French doors and let the girls inside. "Come, young ladies, take your places around the table. Quickly now."

As the girls scrambled for their assigned places, Miss Prudence walked to the head of the table.

"Good morning, young ladies," she said, pausing long enough for the girls to reply. "We are in a hurry this morning, so we will return thanks immediately and have our breakfast."

The girls looked puzzled, then quickly bowed their heads. As soon as the prayer was over, Miss Prudence sat down, and the girls did likewise.

Millie, the maid, poured coffee as usual, but there was no sign of anyone else. When the students had finished their meal, Miss Prudence stayed in the dining room to preside over the second sitting.

"I wonder where Miss Hope is," Mandie said to Celia as they left the dining room. "I didn't see Aunt Phoebe either. Do you think something else has happened?"

"Maybe it has something to do with whatever happened last night," Celia reminded her.

But throughout the morning, the girls went through their classes without catching sight of either Miss Hope or Aunt Phoebe in the hallway. That was unusual. Finally, at the end of one of their classes, Mandie got up the nerve to ask Miss Cameron about it. Miss Cameron came in daily from town to teach.

Mandie and Celia stopped by her desk on the way out of the classroom. "Miss Cameron," Mandie began, "do you know where Miss Hope is, and Aunt Phoebe, too?"

Miss Cameron looked up. "Miss Hope? Why, I suppose she's around somewhere," she replied with a smile. "And Aunt Phoebe is probably busy upstairs."

Mandie immediately realized that her teacher knew nothing about the scene at the supper table the night before. But Miss Cameron listened carefully as Mandie related what happened.

Miss Cameron rose from her desk. "I'm sure that if there were something important going on, Miss Prudence would let everyone know," she replied. "Why don't you two go look for Aunt Phoebe? If she isn't in the kitchen, maybe she's in her house in the backyard."

"That's a good idea." Mandie brightened. "Thanks, Miss Cameron."

The two girls left the classroom and started down the long hallway toward the kitchen.

"Mandie, don't forget," Celia warned. "We're supposed to go to our rooms to study for examinations."

"I know. We'll go upstairs in a minute," Mandie replied. Pushing open the door, she looked into the kitchen, where Millie, all alone, was quickly dishing up food from the big pots on the stove.

Mandie and Celia watched her for a moment from the doorway. "Millie, where is Aunt Phoebe?" Mandie asked.

Millie looked at them absentmindedly. "Lawsy mercy, Missy. Don't bother me. I got to git dis heah food on de table. It be eatin' time any minute now." She quickly went out the other door that connected with the dining room.

Mandie let the big swinging door close as she and Celia stepped back into the hallway. "I suppose if we hurry we could go see if Aunt Phoebe's in her house," she said. Quickly opening the kitchen door again, she hurried across the room to the outside back door.

Celia followed, protesting, "Mandie, you know what'll happen if we get caught roaming around when we're supposed to be studying in our room."

Mandie looked back over her shoulder as she hurriedly opened the back door. "It'll only take a minute. Come on," she urged.

Celia followed, and they ran across the big backyard to the cottage where Aunt Phoebe and Uncle Cal lived. The girls shivered and rubbed their arms in the cold. Neither of them even had a sweater on.

Mandie ran up the steps and knocked loudly on the front door. They stood there a few minutes, knocking and listening, but there was no answer from within. "Let's see if the rig is in the barn," she suggested. Turning around, she ran across the yard to the huge barn where the rig, the smaller surrey, and the horses were kept.

"The surrey is gone!" Mandie exclaimed. "Somebody has gone off in it."

"Let's go back to our room, Mandie," Celia urged her. "It's freezing out here. And someone may see us."

Mandie ran with Celia toward the back door. "I don't believe Miss Hope and Aunt Phoebe and Uncle Cal could all be gone in the surrey," she pondered.

As they burst into the warm kitchen, Millie stood filling the coffeepot for the table. She looked up. "What y'all be doin' out dere in dat cold widdout no wraps?" she scolded.

Mandie and Celia rushed to the big iron cookstove to warm their cold hands. "We're looking for Aunt Phoebe," Mandie answered.

"Well, I tells you right now, you ain't gwine t' find huh. She jes' don't be heah at de moment," Millie said, picking up the filled coffeepot. She turned back as she started through the door to the dining room. "And you bettuh not let Miz Prudence find y'all in heah."

"Wait, Millie," Mandie said anxiously. "Please tell us where Aunt Phoebe is."

"I jes' don't be knowin' dat. All's I knows is I'se havin' to do all huh work dis mornin'." Millie hurried through the door into the dining room.

The girls looked at each other in dismay.

Mandie frowned. "I think she does know where Aunt Phoebe is," she said.

"And she's been told not to tell anyone," Celia added.

"You're right," Mandie agreed, starting for the door to the hallway. "Let's get up to our room before somebody sees us."

The two girls cautiously crept down the long hallway and up the stairs to their room. As they entered their room, the big bell in the backyard began ringing for the noon meal.

Mandie laughed. "I guess we have to turn around and go back down," she said, throwing her books into the chair nearby.

Celia put her books with Mandie's and turned to face the nice warm fire in the fireplace. "I don't know where Aunt Phoebe and Uncle Cal are, but somebody sure is keeping the fires going," Celia said. Turning to the mirror, she gently brushed back some loose tendrils of hair.

"I'm sure it's not Miss Prudence," Mandie added. "Come on, we've got to wash our hands and get downstairs."

After quickly freshening up in the bathroom, the girls rushed down to join the line to the dining room. There, several of the students were trying to guess where Miss Hope and Aunt Phoebe had gone.

Inside the dining room, Miss Prudence presided over their meal as usual and then remained for the second sitting again. After the headmistress dismissed them, Mandie and Celia started to leave with the other girls, but Miss Prudence called to them across the room.

"Amanda, you and Celia come here," she said loud enough that all the girls stopped to listen. Miss Prudence gave them a stern look. "The rest of you are dismissed. Get along now." Her voice softened. "Amanda, I have a message for you."

Mandie anxiously hurried over to the headmistress, with Celia following. "Yes, Miss Prudence?" Mandie said.

The short, thin elderly woman continued. "It seems that your grandmother would like for you and Celia to come for supper tonight."

Mandie nervously smiled, eager to say something but afraid to.

"I gave permission, but only permission to go eat and come right back," Miss Prudence added. "You are to return to your room afterward and study for your examinations. Is that understood?"

"Yes, ma'am," the girls replied in unison.

"Your grandmother's driver, Ben, will pick you up at five o'clock this afternoon. You are to be ready and waiting in the alcove for him," Miss Prudence explained. "That is all. You may go to your room now, but be sure you study. I cannot overemphasize how important these examinations are."

Mandie beamed at the prospect of seeing her grandmother that afternoon. "Thank you, Miss Prudence," she said.

"Thank you, ma'am," Celia echoed.

As soon as they left the dining room, the girls rushed

to their room and did their best to concentrate on their studies. But they kept wishing the time away until at last they got dressed and went downstairs to wait for Ben.

As soon as they sat down in the alcove at the front of the house, the girls heard Ben drive up in the rig. They jumped up and rushed out to greet him.

Urging Ben to hurry the horses, they quickly rode to Mrs. Taft's huge mansion. When they arrived, the girls almost became entangled in their long skirts as they jumped from the rig.

"What fo' y'all be in sech a all-fired hurry, Missies?" the Negro driver asked as he leaped to their assistance.

"Miss Prudence says we have to hurry and eat and rush right back," Mandie explained as she and Celia ran up the steps. "So we're trying to make the most of every minute."

Evidently Ella, the Negro housekeeper, was watching for them because she quickly opened the front door. The girls almost knocked her down in their haste to get to the parlor.

"Sorry, Ella," Mandie apologized, removing her winter coat, hat, and gloves.

"Excuse us, please," Celia added as she handed the maid her wraps.

"Dat's all right," Ella smiled, "but y'all could at leas' act like young ladies now that you s'posed to be learnin' how at dat school." She turned and hung the girls' things on the hall tree.

"We haven't learned everything yet, Ella," Mandie teased. She and Celia headed down the hallway toward the parlor.

Mrs. Taft was sitting by the fireplace reading, while Snowball, Mandie's white kitten, was curled up asleep on the hearth. The old lady looked up and smiled as the girls entered.

Mandie ran to plant a kiss on her grandmother's cheek and give her a hug. Then as Celia smiled and greeted Mrs. Taft, Mandie snatched up her kitten. Snowball stretched, then snuggled on her shoulder.

Mrs. Taft set her book down and rose from her chair. "Since Miss Prudence is so strict about time, I saw to it that supper would be on the table by the time you got here," she announced. "So let's go to the dining room, dears." She led the way.

The three of them sat at one end of the huge table while Snowball curled up in a chair next to his mistress.

Ella and the other maid, Annie, hurriedly served the meal of baked turkey, cranberries, potatoes, turnip greens, corn bread, biscuits, corn pudding, and English peas.

After they had returned thanks, Mandie realized that she had not seen Hilda, the runaway girl Mandie and Celia had found a few months ago. Mrs. Taft had given her a home.

"Where is Hilda, Grandmother?" Mandie asked.

"She's visiting the Mannings for a few weeks," Mrs. Taft explained. "She seems to get along well with their little girl, you know."

Mandie quickly swallowed a bite of potatoes. "Was there some special reason for asking us over for supper tonight?" she asked, her blue eyes twinkling with excitement.

Mrs. Taft smiled. "I don't really need a reason," she answered. "It's just nice to have y'all around now and then. But I would like to ask you something, Amanda," she said. "Have you heard anything from your mother yet about whether or not someone has been found to accompany you to see the President?"

Mandie put down her fork dejectedly. "No, I haven't heard," she said. "It just doesn't look like I'll get to go." She paused a moment, then continued. "If Mother wasn't going to have that baby, she could go with me, but . . ."

"I do know how hard this adjustment is for you, Amanda," her grandmother replied kindly, "but your mother is awfully happy now that she has married your Uncle John. I know she loved your father, too, when he was alive. I realize that now. And your mother and your Uncle John love each other too."

Tears swam in Mandie's blue eyes. Her grandmother had never said much about her daughter marrying John Shaw. Mandie could only guess that she was probably ashamed of the part she had played in separating Mandie's father and mother when Mandie was born.

Blinking back the tears, Mandie said, "I'm glad they got married, too." She sighed. "I just wish the baby had picked some other time to come."

Celia set down her coffee cup suddenly. "Mandie!" she exclaimed. "I just had an idea. Remember that newspaper article we read that said the President is sick? Maybe your friend Joe's father, Dr. Woodard, could go with you and doctor the President."

Mrs. Taft laughed. "No, dear. The President has his own private doctor," she explained. "I don't think he needs Dr. Woodard attending him. As much as we all love Dr. Woodard, he is still just a country doctor. The President's physician is probably better educated and more knowledgeable."

Mandie shook her head slowly. "That wouldn't work anyway, Celia," she told her. "Dr. Woodard has his own patients he has to visit. He couldn't go all the way to Washington and leave them."

"Keep eating while we talk, girls," Mrs. Taft reminded them. "Time is flying."

Mandie and Celia concentrated more on eating then, and soon Ella and Annie were clearing the dishes and bringing in pumpkin chiffon pie for dessert. The girls excitedly dug into it.

"Amanda," Mrs. Taft began again, "*if* you went to Washington, you know that would be a long trip. And since the President asked that you arrive two days before the inauguration, on March first, you would have to leave school at least two days prior to that in order to get there on time."

Mandie listened intently as her grandmother continued.

"And it would take the same amount of time to return, so you would have to miss several days of school."

"Couldn't I make up that time by studying extra hard?" Mandie asked.

"I'd say that would depend on how you do on your mid-year examinations this week," Her grandmother told her.

Celia swallowed a bite of pie. "Oh, but Mandie always makes straight *A*'s," Celia offered.

"I know, dear," Mrs. Taft replied, "but she'd have to do exceptionally well if she wants to convince Miss Prudence."

"I'll probably do all right on the tests," Mandie said, "but what difference will it make? I don't have anyone to go to Washington with me."

"Now, Amanda," Mrs. Taft admonished with a mischievous smile, "you do well on those examinations, and

I'll just see if there isn't some way to rearrange my plans to—"

"Oh, Grandmother, would you?" Mandie interrupted.

"I'm not sure it is even possible to change my plans," Mrs. Taft replied, "so I can't promise anything. My friends and I have already paid for ship accommodations and made other reservations, but I will do my best to find out whether our plans can be changed."

Mandie jumped up and ran around the corner of the table to give her grandmother a big hug. "I knew you'd help me out," she said excitedly.

Mrs. Taft gave her a quick squeeze. "Let's finish our pie, dear." She motioned to the remaining dessert on her granddaughter's plate.

Mandie sat down and quickly finished her dessert, but she was so excited she hardly tasted it or realized what she was doing.

Finishing only a moment after her friend, Celia took a sip of coffee, then set her cup down. "It'll be wonderful if your grandmother can go with you, Mandie, so you won't miss this opportunity to meet the President," Celia told her. "Just think how special that makes you, to be invited to the White House."

Mandie thought for a moment. "I guess it is a special privilege," she agreed.

"I can't wait to tell everyone"—Celia fidgeted in her chair— "Miss Hope and Aunt Phoebe and—"

"Celia," Mandie interrupted her friend, "we can't say anything until it's all settled," she reminded her. "But I just thought of something. We haven't told Grandmother about what's going on at the school."

Celia nodded vigorously, and Mandie proceeded to relate the events concerning the disappearance of Miss

Hope, Aunt Phoebe, and possibly Uncle Cal.

"They are probably away visiting somewhere," Mrs. Taft replied. "In fact, they may be back by the time you two return to school." She paused for a moment listening to the clock chiming in the parlor. "Speaking of school, I'm afraid that was the clock striking seven. I promised Miss Prudence y'all would be back by seven-thirty, so we must break up our dinner party, now, dears."

After sending Ella to have Ben get the rig ready, Mrs. Taft walked to the front hallway with the girls and helped them with their wraps. Snowball followed his mistress and rubbed around her ankles as she slipped into her coat.

"Grandmother," Mandie said eagerly, "when will you know whether you can go with me or not?"

"It will take a little doing, Amanda," Mrs. Taft replied. "And then we will have to get final permission from your mother and Uncle John."

"Oh, Grandmother, please hurry things up," Mandie begged, "or I'll die of suspense."

"Well, the first matter of business is for you to do well on your tests," Mrs. Taft reminded her. "Then we'll take it from there, dear." She bent to kiss her granddaughter and gave Celia a little hug.

"I'll make the highest grades in the school. I promise," Mandie assured her. Then stooping to talk to her kitten, she said, "Now, Snowball, you behave yourself here because you and I and Grandmother are going to visit the President—we hope."

Snowball purred as Mandie stroked his soft white fur, then looked up at her and meowed as though he understood what she was saying.

"You'd better hurry, girls," Mrs. Taft reminded them.

Mandie and Celia quickly said goodbye to her and hurried outside to the waiting rig.

When they arrived back in their warm room at the school, Celia shed her coat. "When can I tell everybody that you're going to see the President, Mandie?" she asked excitedly. "When?"

"Not yet, Celia," Mandie replied, taking off her coat and hanging it beside Celia's in the chifferobe. "We've still got lots of things to work out, but I'm beginning to believe that it will all come true."

## Chapter 3 / Does Uncle Cal Know?

The next day, Wednesday, dragged by. Mandie was so excited about the possibility of her grandmother going with her to Washington that she had trouble studying. But as they sat on the rug by the fire in their room, Celia kept reminding her that if she failed her examinations, she probably would not be allowed to go.

"I don't think I'll actually fail anything," Mandie assured her friend. "I may not make real good grades, but I don't think I'll fail."

Celia held her place in her geography book and looked up. "Remember what your grandmother said," Celia reminded her. "And you promised her you would make the best grades in the school."

"I know." Mandie said, "I'll do my best, but there is so much going on. It'll soon be bedtime, and we still haven't seen Miss Hope, Aunt Phoebe, or Uncle Cal. And we haven't been able to find out what's going on."

"I suppose Miss Prudence is the only one who knows," Celia replied, "and she's certainly not going to tell any of us girls."

"You're right," Mandie agreed, staring at the blazing

fire in the fireplace. "But someone keeps the fires blazing hot, and I don't think Miss Prudence would be doing that."

"What about Millie?" Celia asked.

"I don't think Millie would have time to go all over this three-story house just to keep the fires going when she has to cover Aunt Phoebe's cooking duties, too," Mandie answered. "But since we didn't wake up yesterday morning or today when the fire was built in here, we don't know who did it."

"It seems strange for all of us forty girls—thirty-nine without April—to be here with only Miss Prudence and Millie to keep things going," Celia remarked.

Mandie grinned at her friend. "Oh, but there may be some little elves coming in to help when we're asleep or not looking," she teased.

"I wouldn't doubt that at all," Celia teased back.

Mandie stood up and stretched, tossing her book into the big chair. "I'm going to get ready for bed," she told her friend. "I think maybe I'll get up earlier than usual tomorrow and scan through my history book before we go to breakfast." Going over to the chifferobe, she took down her nightclothes. "That way my mind will be fresher."

Celia stood in front of the fire. "Me too," she decided.

---

Mandie didn't sleep much that night. She felt bad because she was sure that her tossing and turning kept waking Celia. So when the clock on the mantel struck five, Mandie quietly slipped out of bed.

Quickly slipping on her robe, she rolled up her sleeves and went to work, building a fire in the fireplace. It was too early for anyone else to come and start a fire. But

Mandie knew how to do it. Before her father died, she had lived in a log cabin in Charley Gap, North Carolina.

Shoveling out the ashes, she put them in the bucket on the hearth. Then after laying kindling on the firedogs, she covered that with a log from the bin nearby. Taking a match from the holder hanging on the side of the fireplace, she struck it and set the kindling afire. In a few minutes, the flames were roaring up the chimney and warming the room.

After quietly slipping into her clothes, Mandie took the oil lamp from the table by the bed and set it on a small table near the fireplace. She lit it and turned it down low.

Reaching for her history book from the big chair, she curled up on the rug in front of the fireplace to study. Just the thought of time running out made her concentrate harder. In fact, she became so absorbed in the historical events in her textbook that she didn't hear the door open.

"Mawnin', Missy," Uncle Cal said quietly behind her.

Mandie jumped.

"What you been doin', gittin' up and buildin' a fire?" he asked.

Mandie drew a deep breath. "Oh, Uncle Cal, am I glad to see you!"

"Why didn't you wait fo' me to build dat fire, Missy?" the old man asked.

"Because I know how," Mandie replied. "I wanted to get up early to study, so I just went ahead and built a fire because it was cold in here." She frowned slightly. "Where have you been, Uncle Cal?" she asked. "And where is Aunt Phoebe? And Miss Hope?"

Uncle Cal walked over to the fireplace and stirred up the small flames. "One question at a time, Missy," he said. "I ain't been nowhere, and—"

Mandie gasped. "You haven't been anywhere? But we haven't seen you since you brought up my luggage Monday."

"I been right heah in de school," the old Negro replied, "but I'se been right busy tryin' to he'p out ev'ry which a-way."

"Well, where is Aunt Phoebe?" Mandie persisted.

Celia rose up in bed and rubbed her eyes. "Yes, and where's Miss Hope?" she said with a yawn.

"Sorry, Celia," Mandie apologized. "I was trying not to wake you."

"That's all right." Celia rubbed her eyes again. "I need to get up and study, too." She watched Uncle Cal poke at the wood in the fireplace again. "What happened Monday?" she asked him. "Miss Hope came running into the dining room, and then Miss Prudence went out with her. And we haven't seen Miss Hope or Aunt Phoebe—or you either—since then."

Uncle Cal scratched his head. "It's like dis, Missies," he said, glancing from Celia to Mandie and back again. "I'se been fo'bidden to talk 'bout what Miz Prudence call *school bidness*."

Mandie and Celia looked at each other in disbelief.

"But, Uncle Cal," Mandie began, "what's so secretive about where Miss Hope and Aunt Phoebe are?"

Uncle Cal smiled. "Sorry, Missies, I'se gotta go now," he said as he turned to leave the room.

"Is it something bad?" Mandie asked. "Has something bad happened?"

"I done give my word to Miz Prudence dat I won't say nothin' to any of you young ladies," Uncle Cal replied. He opened the door. "I'll try to git by yo' room earlier in de mawnin' to build yo' fire if y'all 're plannin' to git up early agin."

"Thanks, Uncle Cal," Mandie said, "but if I get up before you come by, I'll just build it myself. Besides, you must have an awful lot of work to do right now with Aunt Phoebe gone."

"I'se gotta go now," the old man said, pulling the door closed behind him.

Celia jumped out of bed and quickly dressed and joined her friend on the hearth rug.

Mandie sighed. "At least we know who has been keeping up the fires," she said with a shrug. "But you know, I don't see how we could have missed seeing Uncle Cal since Monday. Today's Thursday."

"I can't think about that now, Mandie," Celia said, picking up her geography book. "I have a one-track mind right now, and I've got to memorize some of this stuff."

"You're right, Celia. I'll be quiet so you can study. I need to memorize some of these history dates, too."

The girls were deep in their studies when the big bell in the backyard began ringing for breakfast.

Mandie reluctantly stood up and put down her history book. "Well, I guess that's all the time we've got now," she said, straightening her long skirt.

Celia agreed and got up to straighten her dress in front of the long mirror in the corner.

"Ready?" Mandie asked as she opened the door. "On to breakfast and then to our history and geography tests! Whew! I'll sure be glad when tomorrow afternoon comes and this is all over with."

Celia followed her friend down the stairs. "And maybe by that time you'll hear from your grandmother about her going to Washington with you," she said.

"Celia, please," Mandie begged, turning around. "Let's don't even mention the word *Washington* until the examinations are over, so my mind won't go wandering."

"I'm sorry for leading your mind astray," Celia teased. "I won't say another word about the trip."

That day and the next, Mandie got through the examinations easier than she thought she would. And Friday, when the results were posted on the bulletin board in Miss Prudence's office, the girls all crowded around to find out how they did.

"Mandie, you're number one!" Celia squealed.

"And look, Celia!" Mandie exclaimed, pointing to the list. "You're number two!"

Mandie and Celia moved back out into the hallway to give the other girls a chance to read the board.

"Celia, there must be some mistake," Mandie said breathlessly as they walked toward the parlor. "How did I make the top grades in the whole school? I don't think it's possible."

"I don't see how I made it to the number-two spot, either," Celia replied.

At that moment Miss Prudence came toward them from the front hallway. "Congratulations, Amanda, Celia!" she said, stopping to greet them. "I knew you young ladies would be two students we would be proud of. Even your mothers didn't come out in the top two positions when they attended this school. We are proud of you. We trust you will keep up the good work."

Speechless with this lavish attention, the girls could only murmur a soft thank you.

"Amanda," Miss Prudence continued, "Ben was just here with a message from your grandmother. She would like for you two young ladies to spend the weekend with her."

Mandie and Celia exchanged glances of delight.

"So I asked Ben to come back about four o'clock," the headmistress went on. "You have my permission to stay until after suppertime Sunday evening. Now run along and get your things ready."

Mandie was so excited she could hardly speak. This meant her grandmother had some news for her one way or another about the Washington trip. "Thank you," Mandie finally managed. "Thank you, Miss Prudence!" Mandie turned and hurried toward the stairs, with Celia following. The girls didn't dare run while the headmistress was watching.

Upstairs in their room, the girls hurriedly crammed things into bags, not paying much attention to what they were taking for the weekend. Long before it was time for Ben to arrive, they were back downstairs, walking back and forth in the alcove and watching through the window.

Suddenly Celia stopped pacing. "Mandie, do you realize it's Friday, and we still haven't seen or heard tell of Miss Hope or Aunt Phoebe?"

Mandie halted. "We're just going to have to do something," she said. "I don't know what, but we've got to find out where they are."

"Have you thought that maybe they aren't coming back anymore?" Celia asked.

"Oh, no, Celia!" Mandie protested. "We've got to have them back. That's all there is to it. They're our friends."

"And Uncle Cal must be staying awfully busy. We never see him anymore either," Celia mused. "What are we going to do?"

"I haven't figured anything out yet, but maybe Grandmother will have some ideas," Mandie told her friend. "We'll discuss it with her—after we discuss the Washington trip!"

Ben arrived promptly at four o'clock, and it didn't take much urging to get him to rush the horses on their way. He was known for his fast driving, that is, by everyone except Mrs. Taft, his employer.

And when they arrived at the mansion this time, Mrs. Taft herself was waiting to open the front door. Hurrying inside, the girls handed their coats and bags to the maid. Then they rushed Mrs. Taft into the parlor and warmed themselves while they eagerly shared their news.

Mandie grabbed Snowball, who was asleep on the hearth. "Grandmother, would you believe it?" she excitedly asked. "I made the highest score in the whole school! And Celia was second."

Celia plopped onto the rug by the hearth as Mrs. Taft sat in an armchair by the fire. But Mandie was too excited to sit.

Mrs. Taft gave her granddaughter an endearing smile and pulled her to her side. "I knew you would," she said. "And you, too, Celia. Congratulations!"

Celia leaned forward to warm her hands by the fire. "Thank you, Mrs. Taft," she replied, looking a little embarrassed.

"I want to tell you something, Amanda," Grandmother began. "Even your mother didn't make it to the top when she attended the Heathwoods' school."

Mandie laughed. "That's what Miss Prudence just told us," she replied, rubbing Snowball's white fur.

"Your mother just never did have the get up and go that you have, Amanda," she said as Mandie finally sat on a low stool beside her.

"Or that you have, Grandmother," Mandie laughed.

"I suppose you're right," Mrs. Taft chuckled. "Your mother is more like your grandfather was—intelligent but quiet and with no desire to take chances."

Celia sat back on her haunches. "My mother didn't do as well as I did, either, according to Miss Prudence," she said.

Mrs. Taft reached out and squeezed the girl's hand. "Well, I know she's going to be proud of you, dear."

"Grandmother, tell us your news," Mandie begged. "We've told you ours."

Mrs. Taft flashed a mischievous smile. "My news can be summed up in three words," she said. "We . . . are . . . going!"

"We're going! We're going!" Mandie danced around the room in excitement while Snowball clutched her shoulder in fright. "We're going! We're going!" Mandie repeated over and over.

Celia tugged at her friend's skirt. "Mandie, now may I tell everybody that you're going to see the President? May I?"

Mandie stopped to consider the question. "I suppose I'd better tell Miss Prudence first," she said.

Mrs. Taft looked up. "You'd better *ask* Miss Prudence first. Remember, she has to give permission for you to take all those days off from school."

"I'm sure she will, Grandmother," Mandie said, "especially since I came out number one on the mid-year examinations."

Mrs. Taft raised her eyebrows. "I'd like to give you a little word of advice," she warned. "Don't ever try to predict what that lady will do. I've known her a long time."

"Well, anyway," Mandie said, flopping down on the rug beside Celia, "tell us all about what you've been doing. How did you break your plans for the trip with your friends?"

"It turned out to be quite a complicated mess. I had to get my friends to let me out of the arrangements," Mrs. Taft explained. "At first they were awfully angry with me, but then I was able to get another friend they knew to take my place for the trip. So after a whole lot of confusion changing names on reservations and so forth, we finally managed to get everything settled."

Mandie felt butterflies in her stomach at the thought of actually being able to make the trip.

"Then just this morning," Grandmother continued, "I received an answer from your mother and your Uncle John giving you permission to go with me. And the Mannings have agreed for Hilda to stay with them while we're gone, so we're all set."

Mandie jumped up and hugged her grandmother. "Oh, thank you, Grandmother. Thank you," she said. "I really appreciate your cancelling your plans so that I could go to Washington. I hope our trip will be worth all this."

"Just you never mind, dear," Mrs. Taft replied, her eyes twinkling. "It is rather cold in Europe this time of year, anyway, so I thought I'd go later. Maybe in the summer, when you could go with me."

Mandie's eyes widened. "Me? Go to Europe with you? Oh, Grandmother, could I? Could I?

"I think your mother and your Uncle John will probably agree," Mrs. Taft replied.

Celia exclaimed, "Oh, Mandie! That would be wonderful for you to get a chance to go to Europe!"

The two girls hugged each other; then Mandie turned back to her grandmother, who was smiling.

"Grandmother, what about Celia?" she asked. "Couldn't she go, too? Please?"

"Of course," Mrs. Taft replied. "I'd love to have Celia

go with us. But we would have to get her mother's permission."

"Oh, thank you, Mrs. Taft!" Celia jumped up and gave the woman a big hug.

"Now we have to do things in an orderly way, girls," Mrs. Taft told them as Celia took her place on the hearth rug again. "First of all, Amanda, I have a letter from your mother for Miss Prudence requesting permission for you to take leave from school. We also need to do some shopping, but since you shouldn't take any extra time away from your studies, I'll go to Raleigh this coming week to shop for both of us."

"But, Grandmother," Mandie protested, "I have so many expensive clothes already. Why do I need anything else?" She set Snowball down, and he immediately jumped into Celia's lap and curled up.

"My dear, you are going to visit the President of the United States," Mrs. Taft reminded her. "And you will meet not only him but his wife and other influential people while we're in Washington." She thought for a moment. "Now, let's see, we will also need a ball gown. I plan to allow you to at least appear at the ball. I know you're only twelve years old, but this may be a once-in-a-lifetime opportunity to meet such people," she explained.

Mandie gasped. "Me? Go to a real ball? Oh, Grandmother, I wouldn't know how to act!"

"That's exactly why you're attending the school you're in, to learn how to act socially. So I suggest that you brush up on all those social graces you've been learning," Mrs. Taft instructed her. "And I don't want you to frighten yourself with thoughts of how society operates in Washington, D.C. I want you to remember that you are your mother's daughter and my granddaughter. And our family is accepted in the highest circles of society."

Mandie's mouth dropped open at her grandmother's bragging. Finally she spoke. "But I am one-fourth Cherokee," she objected. "My other grandmother was full-blooded Cherokee, and I don't think Indians go to things like balls in Washington."

"That makes no difference." Mrs. Taft dismissed her protest. "President McKinley has personally invited you to visit him at the White House, and I'm sure you'll be welcomed with open arms anywhere we wish to go." She smiled. "Now, what kind of ball gown would you like?"

Mandie sighed, then thought for a moment. "Just something that's not too fancy," she replied. "Maybe something blue. But I just wouldn't feel right in stuffy, fancy clothes."

"Blue would be nice, dear," Mrs. Taft agreed. "I'll see what I can come up with. Now, I think you will also need a nice fur cape and—"

"A fur cape?" Mandie interrupted.

"Yes," Mrs. Taft replied. "You have to have a suitable wrap for the new dresses I'm going to buy for you. And I imagine a fur cape will feel good at the inauguration ceremony. As you know, it will be held outdoors."

Ella, the maid, entered the parlor to announce that supper was on the table.

"Come on, girls." Mrs. Taft got up to lead the way into the dining room. "Let's go eat, and we'll continue our conversation at the table."

Behind her grandmother's back, Mandie looked at Celia and sighed. She didn't know a trip to Washington could be so bothersome.

# *Chapter 4 / Where Is Miss Prudence?*

Mandie, Celia, and Mrs. Taft talked the whole weekend about the forthcoming trip to Washington and the future trip to Europe. They stayed up late Saturday, attended church Sunday morning, then returned to Mrs. Taft's house and continued their discussion until after supper when it was time for the girls to return to school.

As Mandie and Celia put on their winter coats in the front hallway, Mandie turned to her friend. "This is one time I'm eager to get back to school," she said excitedly.

Mrs. Taft stood by the door, holding the letter for Miss Prudence that Mandie's mother had written. "Now don't forget, Amanda," she said, handing her the letter. "You should give this letter to Miss Prudence as soon as you get back to school."

Mandie took it and carefully tucked it in her pocket. "Don't worry, Grandmother. I won't forget," she said.

Celia started buttoning her coat. "I'm so glad everything is settled now and I can tell everybody about your trip to see the President."

"Not until I give the letter to Miss Prudence," Mandie cautioned. "Remember, she should be the first one to know."

"That's right, dear," Mrs. Taft agreed. "Be sure Miss Prudence knows first."

After everyone had said their goodbyes, the girls climbed into the rig with their bags and persuaded Ben to rush the horses so they could get back to school fast.

At the school, the girls ran up the front steps carrying their bags and gave the front door a hard shove. Excitedly, they hurried down the hallway toward Miss Prudence's office.

"I can't wait to give this letter to Miss Prudence," Mandie said, leading the way.

As they approached the doorway to the office, they almost knocked Miss Hope down as she came out into the hallway. Mandie and Celia gasped in surprise and dropped their bags.

"Oh, I'm sorry, Miss Hope!" Mandie exclaimed. "Where have you been? We've missed you this past week."

"Please excuse us," Celia added.

The schoolmistress straightened her long dark skirt. "You're excused, young ladies." Miss Hope smiled. "I was in a hurry, too."

"But where have you been, Miss Hope?" Mandie asked.

Miss Hope smoothed back her faded auburn hair and looked from one girl to another. She stood erect. "I'm sorry, but I am in a hurry right now. We'll talk some other time," she said, starting down the hallway.

Mandie and Celia quickly followed.

"I suppose there's some deep, dark secret about where you and Aunt Phoebe have been all week, so I won't ask again," Mandie said. "But where is Miss Prudence? I have a letter for her from my mother."

Miss Hope stopped and looked at Mandie. "My sister is not here today," she said. "She'll probably be back tomorrow sometime. Is there anything I can do for you?"

Mandie's face crumpled in disappointment. "Oh, Miss Hope, this is a very important letter, and I was in a hurry to give it to her." She held up the envelope for the schoolmistress to see. "It's sort of urgent."

"Do you know if it's school business?" Miss Hope asked. "Because if it is, then I can open it and see if I can help you."

Mandie and Celia looked at each other. Celia nodded. Mandie turned and handed the letter to Miss Hope.

The schoolmistress quickly opened the sealed envelope and scanned through the letter. Suddenly she gasped and put her arm around Mandie. "Oh, Amanda, you are going to see the President of the United States! I'm so excited for you!"

Mandie looked up at Miss Hope and smiled. "Then do you think it'll be all right with Miss Prudence if I go?"

Miss Hope looked at her in surprise. "Why, I don't see why not. It isn't every day someone is invited by the President to his inauguration. I think my sister will be just as proud of you as I am."

Mandie looked doubtful. "I don't know, Miss Hope," she said. "But if you don't mind, let's just keep this secret until Miss Prudence comes back and I know for sure that she'll give me permission to leave school."

Miss Hope turned back toward the office. "I'll just lock this letter in her desk drawer until she returns," she said. "But I think you can rest easy. I don't see any problem, dear, and I'll certainly keep this confidential until my sister reads it."

Miss Hope hurried on down the hallway and disappeared into the office. Mandie and Celia stood there for a moment, then picked up their bags and walked slowly toward the stairs.

"Oh, shucks!" Mandie sighed. "Why does Miss Prudence have to be gone? I'm just dying to hear directly from her that I have permission to take those days off from school."

Celia stopped her friend on the stairs. "Mandie, we didn't ask if Aunt Phoebe came back, too," she said.

"You're right," Mandie agreed. She lowered her voice to a whisper. "While we have our coats on, let's just run across the yard to Aunt Phoebe's house and see if she's there."

"It's getting late," Celia reminded her. "I don't see any of the other girls around anywhere. Do we have time before the curfew bell rings?"

Mandie quickly unbuttoned her coat. "Let's see," she said. "I just happen to have my watch on." Pulling back her lapels, she grasped a gold watch hanging on a chain around her neck. She flipped open the cover on the face of the watch and looked up. "It's twenty minutes after eight," she said. "We have plenty of time. Come on." The girls left their bags and ran back down the stairs.

Celia followed Mandie through the empty kitchen, across the backyard, and up to the front door of Aunt Phoebe's house. They stopped. There was no sign of a light in the house, and they couldn't hear a sound.

"I don't believe anybody is home, but we might as well knock now that we're here," Mandie said. She raised her fist and knocked loudly on the front door.

Suddenly a loud scream vibrated through the darkness. The girls grabbed each other and shivered in fright.

"W-what w-was that?" Celia stammered in a whisper.

"I-I don't know," Mandie whispered back. "Did it come from inside the house?"

"L-let's g-go," Celia begged.

But Mandie turned back and pounded on the front door. Immediately another loud scream pierced the air.

The girls gasped and ran back down the porch steps. Just then something came hurtling out from under the porch and raced across the yard.

Mandie stopped and laughed. "It was just a couple of cats chasing each other!" She pointed.

Celia took a deep breath and looked in the direction Mandie was pointing. There by the shrubbery at the back door of the big house sat a huge calico cat.

"Miss Prudence doesn't allow cats here," Mandie said, walking slowly toward the calico. "I wonder where they came from."

"I-I don't know." Celia shivered. "Maybe they're just strays." She followed Mandie toward the back door. "But I do know one thing. I'm going upstairs right now!"

As Mandie came near, the cat gave her a knowing look and scampered away through the darkness.

"I guess you're right," Mandie agreed. "We'd better get up to our room."

Hurrying back inside, the girls picked up their overnight bags on the stairway and ran up to their room.

Celia tossed her coat and bag aside to stand in front of the blazing logs in the fireplace. "Br-r-r!" she shivered again. "I didn't realize it was so cold outside until I felt this nice warm fire."

Mandie hung up her coat, then picked up Celia's and hung it beside hers in the chifferobe. As she joined her friend in front of the fireplace, they stood there quietly for a moment, enjoying the warmth. Then suddenly they heard a faint noise overhead. They looked at each other.

"Did you hear that?" Celia whispered.

"It sounded like something moving in the attic over our room here," Mandie replied.

The girls stood quietly again for a few moments, listening, but there was no more noise.

"It must have been a mouse," Mandie said, sitting down on the rug. "Come to think of it, maybe it's that mouse that was in our room."

Celia sat beside her. "I hope that's all it was," she said. "Remember what a mystery we uncovered the last time we heard noises in the attic?"

"I sure do," Mandie said. "We got into lots of trouble, but it was worth it because we saved Hilda."

Celia said thoughtfully, "I'm glad y'all don't have to take Hilda with you to the White House. She'd probably get into all kinds of trouble."

"I know," Mandie admitted. "I'd sure hate to spend all my time chasing after her. She likes to run off too much. But Hilda wasn't invited, so we couldn't take her anyway—if we get to go."

Celia looked quickly at her friend. "Oh, Mandie, do you really think Miss Prudence won't let you?"

"I just don't know," Mandie said. "I won't sleep all night thinking about it. I hope she gets back early in the morning so I'll know what she has to say."

"April Snow is supposed to be back tomorrow, remember?" Celia reminded her friend. "At least that's what Aunt Phoebe said."

"You're right," Mandie replied, nodding her head. "Aunt Phoebe promised to watch out for April and let us know when she gets back; but since Aunt Phoebe doesn't seem to be around, I guess we'll just have to be on guard ourselves."

The girls sat in front of the fire in silence for a few moments longer. Then finally Celia rose to her feet. "Well, we can't just sit here all night," she said. "We'd better get dressed for bed before we have to blow out the lamps for curfew."

The girls undressed before the warm fireplace, and then put on their nightgowns, robes and slippers.

Mandie had just bent over to straighten her slippers when there was a sudden loud noise overhead. This time it sounded as though someone had dropped something heavy.

"Let's go see!" Mandie said, quickly straightening up. Grabbing the oil lamp, she headed for the door.

"Do we have to?" Celia asked, reluctantly following.

"Come on, Celia," Mandie urged. Carrying the lighted lamp, she led the way up the dark attic stairs just outside their room. When they reached the top, the door to the attic was closed. Mandie carefully pushed it open. There was not a sound in the attic.

Mandie paused at the entrance, holding the lamp high to light up the huge, dark room. Celia clung to her friend's robe.

Mandie turned to her. "I don't see anything," she whispered.

"Let's go back to our room, Mandie," Celia pleaded.

Celia let go of her friend and crouched on the top step as Mandie tiptoed inside the attic and flashed the lamp around the room. All she could see was discarded furniture, boxes, old trunks, and odds and ends. Taking a deep breath for courage, she walked around the attic, looking at everything, but there was nothing that could have made the noise.

Celia held her breath, waiting for something to happen.

Mandie came back to the doorway. "There's nobody in here," she whispered.

"Then let's go," Celia begged.

Mandie led the way down the dark stairs with the lamp in her hand. Celia stayed close behind. As they reached the bottom of the steps, they heard a noise on the servants' stairway nearby.

Mandie stopped and listened, but there was only silence. Then the big bell in the backyard began ringing for ten o'clock curfew.

"Time for lights out," Celia whispered. She rushed ahead of Mandie into the warm room.

Mandie came in behind her and set the lamp on the table by the bed. "Guess I'd better put out the light," Mandie said, and as she puffed at the light her quick eye noticed something in the big chair.

"Look!" Mandie said, pointing to the chair as the flame in the oil lamp jumped and stayed lit.

"Why! our coats are on the chair, and I know you hung them up, Mandie," Celia gasped.

Mandie picked hers up and said, "I know I hung them up. Somebody has been in our room while we've been up in the attic."

Celia immediately stooped and looked under the bed. "What are you doing, Celia?" Mandie asked, watching her.

Celia got up, looked at her, and said, "I just wanted to make sure there was nobody under the bed."

Mandie laughed. "I don't think whoever did this would be foolish enough to stay around and take a chance on our catching them."

"You're right, Mandie," Celia said, sitting down on the rug by the fire.

Mandie dropped her coat back onto the chair with Celia's and joined her friend before the fire.

"If April Snow were back in school, I'd be ready to blame all this on her. I think she'd like to lure us off to the attic and then do some meanness in our room," Mandie said. "But she isn't here so it has to be somebody else."

"But who, Mandie?" Celia asked. "She is the only girl here who won't be friendly with us."

"Just give me time, I'll get it all figured out," Mandie said, rising and stretching. "Let's get into bed. The fire is burning low and it's going to be awfully cold tonight."

They raced for the bed and jumped underneath the warm covers.

"I hope I wake up early so I can look for Miss Prudence," Mandie said, "And I hope she gives me permission to take leave from school."

"If I wake up earlier than you, I'll give you a shake," Celia promised.

"I suppose Uncle Cal will be in to build the fire in the morning," Mandie remarked. "That is, if he is still here—and he might not be, you know. There was nobody in his and Aunt Phoebe's house when we knocked."

"Maybe he was just busy somewhere in the house here fixing fires or something," Celia suggested.

Suddenly there was another noise overhead in the attic. The girls both jumped.

Then Mandie relaxed and said, "That's somebody just trying to get us to leave our room again so they can come in here and do something else. So we'll just stay in bed and disappoint them."

"Thank goodness, Mandie," Celia said, with a sigh of relief. The noise stopped and the girls finally fell asleep.

## *Chapter 5 / Mandie Runs Into Trouble*

The next morning Mandie woke to the ringing of the big bell in the backyard. She sat up and quickly jumped out of bed, furious with herself for not waking earlier. Grabbing her clothes, she hurried to the warmth of the fireplace to dress.

Celia pushed back the covers and slid out of the big bed. "Oh, Mandie," she whined, "neither of us woke up early. I'm sorry." Picking out her clothes, she began dressing for the day.

"That's all right," Mandie replied. "I just wanted to catch Miss Prudence before breakfast if possible."

But when the girls joined the other students in the dining room for breakfast, they found Miss Hope at the head of the table.

"Good morning, young ladies," Miss Hope greeted them with a smile. "My sister has not yet returned. Therefore, I will sit with you and also the next group of girls this morning. Now, let's return thanks."

As Miss Hope thanked the Lord for the meal, Mandie and Celia shut their eyes and nudged each other in perfect communication. After they sat down, Mandie whispered, "Of all things! She's not back yet?"

Obviously afraid to talk at the table, Celia grunted softly in return.

When Mandie glanced across the room, her eyes met April Snow's. *So April is back at school*, she thought.

Celia nudged Mandie again. They both knew.

*I wonder if she was back last night*, Mandie said to herself. *She could have been the one making the noises and the one who put our coats on the chair*. But she knew there was no way to find out.

Mandie tried to smile at April, but the school trouble-maker tossed her long black hair and stared back at her with a mean look on her face.

After the students were dismissed from the table, Mandie heard Miss Hope speak to April.

"We're glad you could come back yesterday, dear," the schoolmistress said. "And we're pleased that things are better at home now, also."

Mandie and Celia stopped at the doorway, listening. But when April saw them, she gave a slight nod to Miss Hope, tossed her long black hair, and hurried out of the room without a word.

Mandie motioned for Celia to follow her, and the two girls wandered into the parlor. They had a few minutes before their first class, so they stood by the fireplace and discussed what they had just heard.

"So, more than likely, it *was* April who was making those noises last night," Celia said.

Mandie nodded, then noticed the newspaper lying on the table nearby. Picking it up, she quickly glanced over the front page. "Look," she said. "President McKinley is still sick."

Celia read over Mandie's shoulder. "It says he is im-

that he would watch over you after your father died. Well, I'd say you need some watching over in this situation."

"I don't really know," Mandie said. "You know how he comes and goes. He usually says he'll see me the next change of the moon. You know how he talks."

"Well, don't give up, Mandie," Celia begged. "We have not even begun to fight yet."

Mandie laughed. "I think the only one who could ever win a fight with Miss Prudence is my grandmother," she said. "She isn't here. And I doubt that even she could win this time. But she should be back home by Friday, so I'll just have to wait."

The next day dragged by because Mandie couldn't keep her mind on her lessons. But on Wednesday, she read in the newspaper that President McKinley was recovering rapidly. She and Celia had been praying for him. Mandie thanked the Lord for answering so quickly.

Throughout the day Mandie did her best to avoid Miss Prudence. She got into the habit of walking through the hallway with her head down so she wouldn't have to face the headmistress.

So on Friday when Miss Prudence dismissed the other girls but asked Mandie to wait, Mandie was worried. Reluctantly, she walked over to the head of the table and stood before the stern-faced woman.

After the other girls had left the room, Miss Prudence began to speak. "Your attitude, Amanda, leaves something to be desired," she said. "What seems to be your problem?"

"I'm sorry, Miss Prudence." Mandie looked at the floor as she spoke. "I'm just . . . just . . . ah . . . unhappy because I won't be able to visit the President."

"Amanda, we teach you young ladies to look people



proving, though," she added.

Mandie pointed to a line farther down. "But it also says he will not be in his office or see anyone this week." She could hear the worry in her own voice.

"But he's improving, Mandie," Celia repeated. "That's what counts."

"I feel so sorry for him. He must be awfully sick," Mandie said. "And I haven't even remembered to pray for him to get well."

"We will tonight," Celia promised.

Mandie fussed and fumed through classes all that day, keeping an eye out for Miss Prudence. But it wasn't until the noon meal was over, with Miss Hope again presiding, that Mandie and Celia caught sight of Miss Prudence. Every spare moment, they hung around the parlor, hoping to keep up with what was going on. Finally they spotted Miss Prudence walking down the hallway with her hat and coat on.

Mandie was so excited she ran out into the hallway and followed Miss Prudence down to her office.

Arriving at the doorway just as Miss Prudence was removing her hat and coat, Mandie greeted the headmistress. "Good afternoon, Miss Prudence," she said. "Could I please talk to you for a minute, please?"

Miss Prudence hung her wraps on the nearby coat tree, then turned to face Mandie. She looked as though she had not slept for days.

"Amanda, I've just come in," Miss Prudence said with a sigh. "Couldn't it wait?"

Mandie lingered in the doorway with Celia close behind. "I'm afraid that if it waits much longer, it'll be too late," Mandie replied.

Miss Prudence scowled. "Come on in then," she said.

Mandie entered the office and stood before the desk as the headmistress sat behind it. Celia stayed outside the door, but Mandie was sure she would be listening to every word.

Miss Prudence looked up at Mandie with irritation. "Now what is it, Amanda? Let's hurry up."

"It's like this," Mandie began. "You have a letter from my mother. I gave it to Miss Hope last night because you weren't here. She locked it up in the drawer there in the desk."

Mandie waited while Miss Prudence took a ring of keys from her purse and unlocked the drawer. "I suppose this is it," the headmistress remarked, taking out the letter addressed to her. "Did my sister open this?"

"Yes, ma'am," Mandie replied. "I told her it was school business, so she said she'd open it."

Miss Prudence pulled the sheet of paper out of the envelope and read it. Then looking up, she said, "So you are waiting to see my reaction to this news about a trip to Washington, is that it? Well, I can tell you right now, you will not be allowed to take that much time off from school."

Mandie's heart sank. "Miss Prudence, please let me be excused," she pleaded. "I can go there and back in a hurry. I won't waste any time."

"No, Amanda. That's final," Miss Prudence said adamantly. "There is no need for any further discussion." Standing, she dropped the letter back in the drawer and locked it. "Your education is more important than a visit to the President."

"But, Miss Prudence, this would be an education, too," Mandie persisted. "I would make up all the work I miss, I promise. I'll even take my school books with me and study while I'm gone. Please?"

"Amanda, you may not be aware of it, but no stu is allowed that much time away from school without ing the grade," Miss Prudence said sternly. "Now I h work to do. You are dismissed. Get on with your sched for the day."

"Yes, Miss Prudence." Mandie barely got the word out through the tears that were choking her throat.

As Mandie left the office, Celia rushed to her side. "Don't give up, Mandie," she comforted. "There must be something we can do so you can go to Washington."

When they reached their room and shut the door, Mandie flung herself onto the bed and cried as though her heart would break.

Celia sat down beside her friend. "Mandie, this is not like you," she said. "You've always told me that where there's a will, there's a way."

As Mandie sat up, Celia rushed to the bureau and got her a handkerchief.

"You're right, Celia," Mandie agreed, wiping her swollen eyes. "There must be some way."

"Talk to your grandmother," Celia suggested.

"But Grandmother is gone for the week. She's shopping in Raleigh, remember?" Mandie said. "She's buying clothes for a trip we can't even make." The tears began to roll down her cheeks again.

"Get word to your mother, then," Celia offered.

"It would take so long to get word to my mother that by the time I got an answer, it'd be too late to go t Washington," Mandie sobbed. "I have to answer Preside McKinley's invitation soon."

"What about Uncle Ned?" Celia asked. "When is coming to see you? Remember, he promised your f

in the eye when you talk to them. Now I want to see you do that," Miss Prudence ordered.

Mandie looked up slowly.

"You might as well forget about the trip to see that man in Washington. And if you don't start behaving better, I'll cancel your visits to your grandmother's house. Do you understand?"

"Yes, Miss Prudence," Mandie replied. "I promise I'll do better."

"All right, then," Miss Prudence said with finality. "You may go to your grandmother's this afternoon for the weekend. And please tell Celia that she has my permission as well. Ben will come for you at four o'clock."

Instantly Mandie perked up. Her grandmother must be back from Raleigh. Mrs. Taft could help persuade Miss Prudence. "Thank you, ma'am. Thank you," Mandie said excitedly. "I'll tell Celia. Thank you so much."

"You may go now and get your things ready." With that Miss Prudence dismissed her. "But don't forget what I said," she added.

Mandie hurried out of the dining room to find Celia waiting for her in the parlor.

Celia jumped up. "Well?"

"Grandmother is back!" Mandie announced excitedly. "She's sending Ben for us at four o'clock, and Miss Prudence said you could go, too."

Celia squealed with delight, and the girls headed for their room to get ready. As they gathered the things they would need and crammed them into their bags, Celia looked around the room. "I hope nobody comes in here and bothers anything while we're gone—somebody like April Snow!"

"That must have been her in the attic that night,"

Mandie agreed. "And then when we went up there, as she knew we would, she came in here and put our coats on the chair."

"We haven't heard any more noise, and nobody has bothered anything else since then," Celia added.

"I wish Aunt Phoebe would come back. She could watch April Snow for us while we're gone," Mandie said. "You know, it's strange that no one will say anything about Aunt Phoebe. She's been gone almost two weeks. But since Miss Hope and Miss Prudence have been staying around, maybe Aunt Phoebe is doing something for them."

"I don't know," Celia replied. "Uncle Cal won't even talk about it."

"Come on. Let's go downstairs," Mandie urged. "We can watch for Ben better sitting in the alcove than we can up here."

Ben came on time, and when they arrived at Mrs. Taft's mansion, she was waiting for them.

"Oh, my dears," she said, leading them into the parlor, "I'm so glad to see you both. Amanda, I have so much to show you. I just bought and bought. There were so many pretty things that I couldn't decide what to get for you, so I just bought everything I thought you would like, and—"

"Grandmother," Mandie interrupted. "Miss Prudence won't let me out of school to make the trip."

Mrs. Taft's mouth opened wide, and she just stood there in shock for a few moments before lowering herself into a chair by the fire. The girls plopped down on the hearth rug, and Mandie related what had happened.

Mrs. Taft bristled in her chair. "Just who does that woman think she is?" she said angrily. "You are going to

proving, though," she added.

Mandie pointed to a line farther down. "But it also says he will not be in his office or see anyone this week." She could hear the worry in her own voice.

"But he's improving, Mandie," Celia repeated. "That's what counts."

"I feel so sorry for him. He must be awfully sick," Mandie said. "And I haven't even remembered to pray for him to get well."

"We will tonight," Celia promised.

Mandie fussed and fumed through classes all that day, keeping an eye out for Miss Prudence. But it wasn't until the noon meal was over, with Miss Hope again presiding, that Mandie and Celia caught sight of Miss Prudence. Every spare moment, they hung around the parlor, hoping to keep up with what was going on. Finally they spotted Miss Prudence walking down the hallway with her hat and coat on.

Mandie was so excited she ran out into the hallway and followed Miss Prudence down to her office.

Arriving at the doorway just as Miss Prudence was removing her hat and coat, Mandie greeted the headmistress. "Good afternoon, Miss Prudence," she said. "Could I please talk to you for a minute, please?"

Miss Prudence hung her wraps on the nearby coat tree, then turned to face Mandie. She looked as though she had not slept for days.

"Amanda, I've just come in," Miss Prudence said with a sigh. "Couldn't it wait?"

Mandie lingered in the doorway with Celia close behind. "I'm afraid that if it waits much longer, it'll be too late," Mandie replied.

Miss Prudence scowled. "Come on in then," she said.

Mandie entered the office and stood before the desk as the headmistress sat behind it. Celia stayed outside the door, but Mandie was sure she would be listening to every word.

Miss Prudence looked up at Mandie with irritation. "Now what is it, Amanda? Let's hurry up."

"It's like this," Mandie began. "You have a letter from my mother. I gave it to Miss Hope last night because you weren't here. She locked it up in the drawer there in the desk."

Mandie waited while Miss Prudence took a ring of keys from her purse and unlocked the drawer. "I suppose this is it," the headmistress remarked, taking out the letter addressed to her. "Did my sister open this?"

"Yes, ma'am," Mandie replied. "I told her it was school business, so she said she'd open it."

Miss Prudence pulled the sheet of paper out of the envelope and read it. Then looking up, she said, "So you are waiting to see my reaction to this news about a trip to Washington, is that it? Well, I can tell you right now, you will not be allowed to take that much time off from school."

Mandie's heart sank. "Miss Prudence, please let me be excused," she pleaded. "I can go there and back in a hurry. I won't waste any time."

"No, Amanda. That's final," Miss Prudence said adamantly. "There is no need for any further discussion." Standing, she dropped the letter back in the drawer and locked it. "Your education is more important than a visit to the President."

"But, Miss Prudence, this would be an education, too," Mandie persisted. "I would make up all the work I miss, I promise. I'll even take my school books with me and study while I'm gone. Please?"

"Amanda, you may not be aware of it, but no student is allowed that much time away from school without failing the grade," Miss Prudence said sternly. "Now I have work to do. You are dismissed. Get on with your schedule for the day."

"Yes, Miss Prudence." Mandie barely got the words out through the tears that were choking her throat.

As Mandie left the office, Celia rushed to her side. "Don't give up, Mandie," she comforted. "There must be something we can do so you can go to Washington."

When they reached their room and shut the door, Mandie flung herself onto the bed and cried as though her heart would break.

Celia sat down beside her friend. "Mandie, this is not like you," she said. "You've always told me that where there's a will, there's a way."

As Mandie sat up, Celia rushed to the bureau and got her a handkerchief.

"You're right, Celia," Mandie agreed, wiping her swollen eyes. "There must be some way."

"Talk to your grandmother," Celia suggested.

"But Grandmother is gone for the week. She's shopping in Raleigh, remember?" Mandie said. "She's buying clothes for a trip we can't even make." The tears began to roll down her cheeks again.

"Get word to your mother, then," Celia offered.

"It would take so long to get word to my mother that by the time I got an answer, it'd be too late to go to Washington," Mandie sobbed. "I have to answer President McKinley's invitation soon."

"What about Uncle Ned?" Celia asked. "When is he coming to see you? Remember, he promised your father that he would watch over you after your father died. Well, I'd say you need some watching over in this situation."

"I don't really know," Mandie said. "You know how he comes and goes. He usually says he'll see me the next change of the moon. You know how he talks."

"Well, don't give up, Mandie," Celia begged. "We have not even begun to fight yet."

Mandie laughed. "I think the only one who could ever win a fight with Miss Prudence is my grandmother," she said. "She isn't here. And I doubt that even she could win this time. But she should be back home by Friday, so I'll just have to wait."

The next day dragged by because Mandie couldn't keep her mind on her lessons. But on Wednesday, she read in the newspaper that President McKinley was recovering rapidly. She and Celia had been praying for him. Mandie thanked the Lord for answering so quickly.

Throughout the day Mandie did her best to avoid Miss Prudence. She got into the habit of walking through the hallway with her head down so she wouldn't have to face the headmistress.

So on Friday when Miss Prudence dismissed the other girls but asked Mandie to wait, Mandie was worried. Reluctantly, she walked over to the head of the table and stood before the stern-faced woman.

After the other girls had left the room, Miss Prudence began to speak. "Your attitude, Amanda, leaves something to be desired," she said. "What seems to be your problem?"

"I'm sorry, Miss Prudence." Mandie looked at the floor as she spoke. "I'm just . . . just . . . ah . . . unhappy because I won't be able to visit the President."

"Amanda, we teach you young ladies to look people

in the eye when you talk to them. Now I want to see you do that," Miss Prudence ordered.

Mandie looked up slowly.

"You might as well forget about the trip to see that man in Washington. And if you don't start behaving better, I'll cancel your visits to your grandmother's house. Do you understand?"

"Yes, Miss Prudence," Mandie replied. "I promise I'll do better."

"All right, then," Miss Prudence said with finality. "You may go to your grandmother's this afternoon for the weekend. And please tell Celia that she has my permission as well. Ben will come for you at four o'clock."

Instantly Mandie perked up. Her grandmother must be back from Raleigh. Mrs. Taft could help persuade Miss Prudence. "Thank you, ma'am. Thank you," Mandie said excitedly. "I'll tell Celia. Thank you so much."

"You may go now and get your things ready." With that Miss Prudence dismissed her. "But don't forget what I said," she added.

Mandie hurried out of the dining room to find Celia waiting for her in the parlor.

Celia jumped up. "Well?"

"Grandmother is back!" Mandie announced excitedly. "She's sending Ben for us at four o'clock, and Miss Prudence said you could go, too."

Celia squealed with delight, and the girls headed for their room to get ready. As they gathered the things they would need and crammed them into their bags, Celia looked around the room. "I hope nobody comes in here and bothers anything while we're gone—somebody like April Snow!"

"That must have been her in the attic that night,"

Mandie agreed. "And then when we went up there, as she knew we would, she came in here and put our coats on the chair."

"We haven't heard any more noise, and nobody has bothered anything else since then," Celia added.

"I wish Aunt Phoebe would come back. She could watch April Snow for us while we're gone," Mandie said. "You know, it's strange that no one will say anything about Aunt Phoebe. She's been gone almost two weeks. But since Miss Hope and Miss Prudence have been staying around, maybe Aunt Phoebe is doing something for them."

"I don't know," Celia replied. "Uncle Cal won't even talk about it."

"Come on. Let's go downstairs," Mandie urged. "We can watch for Ben better sitting in the alcove than we can up here."

Ben came on time, and when they arrived at Mrs. Taft's mansion, she was waiting for them.

"Oh, my dears," she said, leading them into the parlor, "I'm so glad to see you both. Amanda, I have so much to show you. I just bought and bought. There were so many pretty things that I couldn't decide what to get for you, so I just bought everything I thought you would like, and—"

"Grandmother," Mandie interrupted. "Miss Prudence won't let me out of school to make the trip."

Mrs. Taft's mouth opened wide, and she just stood there in shock for a few moments before lowering herself into a chair by the fire. The girls plopped down on the hearth rug, and Mandie related what had happened.

Mrs. Taft bristled in her chair. "Just who does that woman think she is?" she said angrily. "You are going to

Washington, dear. I'll see to that."

"Miss Prudence seems awfully determined that I'm not going," Mandie replied.

"You leave that woman to me!" Mrs. Taft snapped.

---

After dinner, when Mrs. Taft displayed the products of her shopping trip, Mandie was impressed with all the beautiful clothes, but her heart wasn't in it. Her grandmother didn't seem to notice her dull interest, partly because Celia kept oohing and aahing over everything.

Finally Mandie just said, "Grandmother, I wish there were some way to settle all this with peace."

Mrs. Taft looked at her granddaughter, puzzled. "Why, there is, my dear. We can always transfer you to another school."

Mandie gasped in shock. "Another school?"

Celia drew a sharp breath.

"Yes, dear. Miss Prudence's school isn't the only one around. There are lots of other nice girls' schools where you could go," Mrs. Taft explained.

"Oh, Mandie!" Celia cried, "please don't go to another school and leave me to deal with April Snow all alone."

Before Mandie could reply, Mrs. Taft continued, "That's what I plan on suggesting to your mother, dear, if we can't get Miss Prudence to change her mind. But there is one thing for sure. You *are* going to Washington. I'll get a message to your mother right away."

Mandie silently looked at her grandmother. Why did her happiness over the invitation have to get all fouled up?

"It takes so long to get messages back and forth, I think I'll have one of those telephones put in the house here, and I'll see that Elizabeth gets one, too." Mrs. Taft looked at her granddaughter, expecting a remark about that, but Mandie was silent. "Don't worry, dear," Grandmother said. "I'm sure your mother will back us up."

Mandie's mind was in turmoil now. In order to go on that wonderful visit to see the President, other people were getting angry. It made her sad.

---

Mandie and Celia returned to school after supper Sunday with Mrs. Taft's promise to send word as soon as she heard from Mandie's mother, Elizabeth Shaw. "Don't worry," she had said. "You just continue on with your studies, and I'll make sure you get to Washington."

As Mandie and Celia entered the school that night, Miss Prudence was coming down the hall. But when she saw them, she quickly turned around and went back into her office.

Mandie frowned. *Is Miss Prudence trying to avoid me now?* she wondered. "Well," she said with a sigh, "I suppose we can just go on up to our room."

Celia nodded and the girls headed upstairs. There was no one else around. Evidently all the other girls were already in their rooms for the night. In the wintertime the weather was usually too bad for outdoor activities. Everyone had a habit of gathering in one another's rooms throughout the school.

Mandie and Celia spent most of their time with just each other. They were friendly with the other girls but hadn't developed any other close friendships.

When they reached their room, they sat on the rug by the fire to talk for awhile. Celia turned to her friend. "You look sad, Mandie," she observed. "Are you worried that you may have to go to another school?"

Mandie stared into the bright flames and thought for a moment. "No, Celia," she replied. "I'm not worried about that. I think I'd give up the trip to Washington rather than have to change schools. You know how much I hate being away from my mother in this school anyway. It would be terrible if I had to go to a new school where I didn't know anybody."

"You would give up the trip to Washington?" Celia asked in amazement.

"I certainly don't want to, but if I have to, I will," Mandie said. "Everything has been against my going ever since I received the invitation, and I'm tired of it. There's just been too much trouble and hard feelings."

"I do hope everything works out," Celia said. "It's such an important event in your life. Besides, I think even President McKinley will be disappointed if you don't go."

Mandie laughed and stood up. "I'm sure it won't make any difference to him. He was just being nice to me when he offered the invitation." She stretched and yawned. "It must be about time for the bell. Let's get ready for bed."

Suddenly there was a noise in the attic. The girls glanced at each other and froze.

"Let's ignore it," Mandie said when the noise finally stopped. "I think somebody's just doing it to get us out of our room."

"Probably," Celia agreed.

After they had slipped into their nightgowns and jumped into bed, Mandie blew out the light. "Let's not forget to pray for the President," she reminded her friend.

"And we'll keep praying that everything will work out for you to go to Washington," Celia replied.

The next morning when Mandie found the newspaper

in the parlor, she was happy to read that President McKinley had recovered and was back in his office.

But then on Wednesday morning when the girls glanced through the paper, they read that Queen Victoria had died the evening before. Her son, King Edward VII, was to take title that day.

"How sad," Mandie said. "Just when our President gets well, England's queen dies."

"Yes," Celia said, reading over her friend's shoulder. "Let's read all the details. This will probably be part of our history lesson today."

Later that day, when their teacher brought up the subject, Mandie and Celia were the only ones who knew anything about it. Most of the other students never bothered to read the newspaper.

On Friday the girls again went to Mrs. Taft's house for the weekend. And on Saturday Uncle Ned, Mandie's old Cherokee friend, arrived. Ella, the maid, ushered him into the parlor where Mrs. Taft and the girls were sitting.

"Come on in by the fire, Uncle Ned," Mrs. Taft invited.

Mandie ran to greet him and held his old wrinkled hand, leading him over to the warm fireplace. "Oh, Uncle Ned, I'm so glad to see you," she said. "How did you know I was here?"

"Not come to see Papoose," Uncle Ned replied. "Come to see grandmother of Papoose." Pulling a large sealed envelope out of his deerskin jacket, he handed it to Mrs. Taft.

Mandie pouted. When Uncle Ned showed up anywhere, it was usually Mandie he was coming to visit. But before she had time to think much about it, her grandmother had ripped open the large envelope and found three smaller envelopes inside.

"Here is a letter from your mother, Amanda," Mrs. Taft said, handing her one of the envelopes. "This one is for me, and the other is addressed to Miss Prudence. Evidently your mother took care of everything."

Mrs. Taft and Mandie hurriedly opened their letters.

Mandie frowned as she read hers silently. "Grandmother," she said, holding up the single sheet of paper, "my letter only says that Mother is sending a letter to Miss Prudence asking that she reconsider her decision."

Mrs. Taft refolded her letter and put it back into the envelope. "I wonder exactly what she has written to Miss Prudence," she said. "It's sealed, but how about going right now to deliver it and find out what she has to say?"

Mandie grinned. "I'm ready," she agreed. "They should be all through with dinner when we get back to the school."

Mrs. Taft stood. "Uncle Ned, you're spending the night, of course," she said. "Have you had supper yet?"

"Eat before sun disappear," Uncle Ned told her, still warming his hands by the fire.

"That was a long time ago," Mrs. Taft replied. "I'll have Ella fix you something while we're gone. We should be back in a few minutes." Excusing herself, she went to find the maid.

Mandie turned to her old Indian friend. "Uncle Ned, you know what's going on, don't you?" she asked.

"Me know." The old man nodded. "Where there's will, there's way. Must not give up, Papoose. "All things be happy again."

Mandie managed a weak smile. "Thank you, Uncle Ned. I hope so."

Celia jumped up from the footstool where she had been sitting. "I'll get our coats and hats, Mandie." Disappearing into the hallway, she returned a few minutes later with their wraps.

Just then Mrs. Taft came back into the room with her hat and coat on. "Uncle Ned, go on back to the breakfast room," she said. "I told Ella to set you a place in there. It's smaller and will be warmer than that big, drafty dining room."

Uncle Ned rose. "Thank you," he said.

Mandie gave her Indian friend a hug. "We'll be right back, Uncle Ned," she told him. "Pray for everything to be all right."

Uncle Ned nodded. "Big God make things happy," he replied.

## *Chapter 6 / Grandmother Confronts Miss Prudence*

When Mrs. Taft and the girls arrived at the school, they found Miss Prudence and Miss Hope sitting in the office doing paperwork.

Mandie's grandmother marched right in and handed the letter to the headmistress. "Here is a letter to you from Amanda's mother," she said, clipping her words short.

Miss Prudence reluctantly took the letter and turned it over. "Thank you," she replied hesitantly.

"We'll wait until you read it," Mrs. Taft responded. Taking a chair nearby, she motioned for the girls to sit down, too.

Miss Prudence looked at her silently, then ripped open the envelope. Her disciplined face showed no emotion as she read the single sheet of paper, then dropped it on the desk in front of her. She looked up. "My answer is the same," she announced. "If Amanda takes leave to go to Washington, she will fail the grade. Even though your daughter was my student, Mrs. Taft, and I know she is an agreeable person, I will not let her plea change my decision."

Miss Hope moved closer and picked up the letter. After reading it, she turned to the headmistress. "But, sister, think what this trip would do for our school," she argued. "It's not very often a school can boast that one of its students was personally invited by the President of the United States to visit the White House."

Miss Prudence turned quickly. "You, sister, are forgetting something." Her voice sounded angry. "That man in the White House is from the wrong political party." She spat out the words.

"I know, but we didn't put him there," Miss Hope protested. "We women can't vote. The men are the ones who elected him. And now that he is there, he *is* President of the United States, whether we like it or not. This would be such good publicity for our school."

Knowing that Miss Hope was on her side, Mandie grabbed Celia's hand hopefully, hardly daring to breathe.

"No." Miss Prudence remained firm. "I don't see what kind of publicity you think we would benefit from. Most people will never know—or care, for that matter—that Amanda was invited to the White House."

"But we could see that the newspaper wrote about it," Miss Hope said. "Not only that, the other girls here live in various parts of the country, and word would spread that way."

Miss Prudence did not answer right away. Mrs. Taft bristled in her chair and Mandie's heart beat faster as they all waited to hear what the headmistress would say.

During the lull in the conversation, Mandie happened to catch sight of Aunt Phoebe at the doorway. She was so excited that she jumped up and ran to hug the old woman. "Oh, Aunt Phoebe, we're so glad you're back!" she cried, holding on to the old black woman's sleeve.

"We've missed you so much."

"Why, I'se glad to be back, Missy," Aunt Phoebe said tenderly. Then quickly turning to the headmistress, she said, "I'se sorry, Miz Prudence. I didn't knows you had comp'ny in here." She turned to go.

Miss Prudence looked up. "What did you want, Aunt Phoebe?" she asked.

Aunt Phoebe looked back. "I jes' wanted to make my 'port on de latest 'velopments out at de farm," she replied. "I comes back later." Again she turned to leave.

*So*, Mandie said to herself, *this whole disappearance mystery has something to do with the farm. . . .* Mandie knew Aunt Phoebe was talking about the farm where some of Uncle Cal's relatives lived and raised food for the school. If the disappearances had something to do with the farm, that would explain why Uncle Cal and Aunt Phoebe were involved. *But what could have happened?* she wondered.

Miss Prudence's voice interrupted her thoughts. "Fine, Aunt Phoebe. Please come back in a few minutes," she said. As the old Negro woman left, Miss Prudence looked directly at Mandie's grandmother. "I believe we have finished our conversation, Mrs. Taft. Now, if you don't mind, my sister and I have work to do." She stood up, indicating there was nothing more to discuss.

Everyone else stood as well.

Mandie's grandmother straightened her shoulders. "Very well, then, Miss Prudence. I will take up the matter with my daughter again, and we will let you know what we decide to do. But we just may not be able to support your school any longer."

Miss Hope looked pleadingly at her sister, but Miss Prudence ignored her.

"If you no longer choose to be a patron of our school, that is certainly your right," Miss Prudence remarked haughtily. "We have a great many others. Good night."

Mandie gave Miss Hope a wishful glance. The headmistress's sister was never aggressive, but when she believed in something, she was relentless. Mandie was counting on that.

Mrs. Taft pulled her fur coat about her. "Good night, Miss Prudence," she said, turning to leave. "Come, girls. Let's go home."

Miss Prudence stepped around to the front of the desk. "Amanda and Celia, you will be expected back here tomorrow night before curfew." She looked at them sternly as she spoke.

"Yes, Miss Prudence," the girls replied together.

Miss Hope followed them out into the hallway. Bending slightly, she squeezed Mandie's hand and whispered, "I'll keep trying."

Mandie's heart was thumping wildly. "Thank you, Miss Hope," she said.

As Mrs. Taft took the girls back home with her in the buggy, she fussed all the way. "I don't know who that woman thinks she is, refusing to allow *my* granddaughter to take a few days off from school," she mumbled as Ben drove the buggy through the cobblestone streets of Asheville.

Mandie laid her hand on her grandmother's. "I'm sorry I've caused so much trouble, Grandmother," she said.

"You didn't cause any trouble, dear," Mrs. Taft replied, patting Mandie's hand. "It's that obstinate woman who runs your school. But I promise you we'll do something about it."

Hearing her grandmother say that didn't make Mandie feel any better. She was worried.

As soon as they arrived at Mrs. Taft's house, Mandie motioned for Celia to come to the bathroom with her. Quietly closing the door behind them, Mandie began to whisper. "Celia, would you please do me a favor?" she asked.

Celia looked bewildered. "What?"

"Grandmother went into the parlor, and I think Uncle Ned is in there. I'm worried about what my grandmother might do about all this, and I want a chance to talk things over with Uncle Ned," Mandie explained. "Would you please keep my grandmother talking or something so I can speak to Uncle Ned privately?"

"I'll try," Celia promised. "Your grandmother is pretty wound up. I'm not sure she'll pay any attention to me."

"Go ahead into the parlor," Mandie urged. "Then I'll come to the doorway and ask Uncle Ned if I could talk to him for a few minutes in the sun parlor. When I do this, you start talking to my grandmother about the trip to Washington. She has a one-track mind, and right now Washington, D.C., is all she's thinking about. Besides, I do need to talk to Uncle Ned about the hospital we're building for the Cherokees. Will you do it? Please?"

"All right." Celia opened the door. "But please don't blame me if this doesn't work," she warned, heading out to the parlor.

Mandie waited a few minutes, then went and stood at the doorway to the parlor. Uncle Ned sat by the fire while Celia carried on a rapid conversation with Mandie's grandmother. Uncle Ned looked up.

Mandie motioned to him. "May I talk to you a few minutes, Uncle Ned?" she asked softly. Turning, she headed down the hallway, and her Cherokee Indian friend followed.

Inside the sun parlor, Uncle Ned looked at Mandie with concern. "What bother Papoose?" he asked.

Mandie sat on the settee by the fire, and Uncle Ned joined her. "I just wanted to tell you I'm worried about the way my grandmother has been acting," Mandie began.

"Ned understand, Papoose." The old Indian took her small white hand in his old wrinkled one. "I see worry in Papoose. I wanted talk, too." He smiled warmly. "I know grandmother of Papoose many year. Always talk big, but big talk just big blow. Big blow soon blow away. She want big things for Papoose. Not want other people interfere."

"But, Uncle Ned," Mandie replied, looking up into his piercing black eyes, "I'd rather not go to Washington at all than have everybody angry."

"Miss Head Lady, she big blow, too. Two big blows meet and blow go away," the old Indian explained. "Everything be all right, Papoose. Big God look after Papoose. Trust Big God fix everything."

"I do trust God, Uncle Ned," Mandie assured him. "I'll talk to Him about Grandmother tonight when I say my prayers."

"That right thing," the Indian replied. "If Big God want Papoose to go, Papoose will see President man in Big City."

"I hope so very much, Uncle Ned," Mandie said. She began to relax a little. "Oh," she said after a moment, "I almost forgot. I need to know what has been done on the hospital so I can tell President McKinley. You know, that's the reason he invited me, because of the hospital."

"Hospital be ready when air get warm, trees get green," he told her. "Much work done now. Doctor man tell men hurry." A smile teased at Uncle Ned's mouth.

Mandie smiled back. "I knew Dr. Woodard would keep after everyone to finish it," she replied. "I know I can't do anything about the project while I'm here at school. But I will be glad when it's finished, so all the Cherokees who get sick can go there for help. Dr. Woodard said he would spend a lot of time there himself, doctoring them." Looking up, Mandie saw Celia at the doorway.

Celia shrugged and made a face. "It didn't work too good, Mandie," she apologized. "Your grandmother sent me to tell you and Uncle Ned to come back into the parlor. She wants to know about the Cherokee hospital, too. And she wants to send a message by Uncle Ned to your mother when he goes back tomorrow."

Mandie sighed and followed Uncle Ned and Celia back to the parlor.

Mrs. Taft didn't say exactly what kind of a message she was sending back to Mandie's mother with Uncle Ned, but Mandie could imagine what it was. She was going to suggest that Elizabeth Shaw take Mandie out of Miss Prudence's school.

When Mandie and Celia got ready for bed that night in Mrs. Taft's huge guest room, they both knelt by the high bed and said their prayers. Mandie talked to God about her grandmother and Miss Prudence, and Celia pleaded that Mandie not be taken out of the Heathwoods' School for Girls.

The next morning, Sunday, they all got up in time to go to church. Mandie and Celia followed Mrs. Taft to their pew. Looking around, Mandie saw Miss Prudence and Miss Hope across the aisle with the other girls from school. Mandie, feeling guilty about the conflict with Miss Prudence, quickly turned her head before the headmistress could look at her.

All during the service, Mandie was aware of Miss Prudence across the aisle, and it was hard for Mandie to keep her mind on the music and sermon. When the service was over and everyone got up to leave, Miss Prudence told the other students to wait for her in the rig, and she turned back to block Mrs. Taft's path. Mandie's heart thumped loudly.

"It's a nice day, isn't it, Mrs. Taft?" Miss Prudence began.

"Yes, I believe it is." Mrs. Taft stopped in the aisle, her way blocked.

"Mrs. Taft, I need to apologize to you," she said, trying to keep her tone businesslike.

Mandie couldn't believe her ears. Miss Prudence apologizing?

Mrs. Taft started to speak, but the headmistress held up her hand and shook her head. "No, please, let me finish. There have been some difficult developments at the school recently, and . . ."

Mandie desperately wanted to ask what those mysterious developments were, but she didn't dare interrupt.

Miss Hope came up and put her hand on the headmistress's shoulder. "My sister has been under a great deal of strain," she explained.

Miss Prudence continued. "I must admit I let my own political leanings keep me from making a rational decision." She fidgeted with the white gloves she held in her hand. "But I wanted to let you know that I have thought things over and have decided that perhaps a trip to Washington, D.C., might be quite educational for Amanda."

Mandie's face lit up.

"She will be excused to make the trip to Washington—that is, *if* she promises to study while she is away and *if* she does not take any more leave time this year."

Mandie nodded her head vigorously, and before Mrs. Taft could open her mouth to reply, Mandie was practically jumping up and down. "Thank you, Miss Prudence. Thank you!" she cried over and over.

Mrs. Taft smiled triumphantly. "I'm so glad," she said. "I suppose I owe you an apology as well." She straightened her skirt self-consciously. "Thank you for reconsidering. We'll be planning the details of the trip then."

Miss Prudence looked at Mandie. "Amanda, you heard me," she warned as she put on her gloves. "You have to promise to take your books with you and to study diligently while you are gone."

Mandie at once became calm. "Yes, Miss Prudence. I do indeed promise," she replied in a proper, ladylike voice. "I'm just so happy to be able to visit the President."

Mrs. Taft put her hand on her granddaughter's shoulder. "I will see that she studies," she assured the headmistress. "Come, dears." She motioned to Mandie and Celia. "It's time to go home for dinner." They all stepped out onto the front steps of the church.

Mandie turned and looked up into the headmistress's eyes. "Thank you again, Miss Prudence," she said sincerely. "We'll see you later tonight."

To Mandie's astonishment, Miss Prudence actually waved a gloved hand and smiled as Mandie stepped into the rig where Ben waited for them.

"I wish Uncle Ned hadn't left so early this morning so I could tell him the good news," Mandie said excitedly.

"Uncle Ned had to visit some friends over in the mountains," Mrs. Taft told her. "So I asked him to stop by on his way back through tomorrow morning and I'd give him a note for your mother. I'll tell him for you since you'll be back at school by then."

"Thanks, Grandmother," Mandie answered.

Celia, who had not said a word until now, tugged on Mandie's coat sleeve. "May I tell everybody now, Mandie? Is it all right to tell people that you're going to visit the President? Please?"

Mandie paused a moment. "Well, actually, Celia," she remarked, "I think *I'd* like to be the one to spread the word." She barely noticed the hurt look Celia gave her.

As soon as they got back to Mrs. Taft's house, Mandie asked if she could borrow some of her grandmother's stationery. "I want to send President McKinley my reply right away," she said as they hung their wraps on the coat tree in the front hallway.

"Of course, dear, but I think we should have dinner first," Mrs. Taft replied, leading the way to the dining room.

The servants in Mrs. Taft's household were all expected to attend church on Sunday. Dinner was cooked the day before, then reheated and placed on the table for everyone to help themselves. The servants ate in the kitchen. After the meal was finished, the servants took away the used dishes and draped an extra white linen tablecloth over the food, saving it for supper.

Mandie and Celia followed Mrs. Taft to the long table where the food and dishes were already laid out. Mrs. Taft took a china plate from the short stack at one end of the table and began filling her plate. "Help yourselves, girls," she offered. "Then sit down at the other end there where we can talk."

The girls hungrily dug into the various bowls and platters and carried their heaping plates to the places Mrs. Taft indicated.

After a brief prayer of thanks, Mrs. Taft began telling Mandie her ideas. "In your letter to the President, Amanda, you should inform him that your grandmother will be traveling with you, so he can make proper arrangements at the White House."

"Of course, Grandmother," Mandie said between bites of juicy country ham. "I'm sure he wouldn't expect me to come alone. I'm planning to take Snowball with me, too."

"Oh, Amanda. I'm not sure we can handle that cat on the trip," Mrs. Taft replied doubtfully. "Why don't you just leave him here?"

"But, Grandmother," Mandie protested, "it isn't every day that a cat is allowed to visit the President. I'll take care of him."

As Celia cut her meat, she turned to her friend. "Mandie," she said, "when Uncle Ned comes by tomorrow on his way home, why don't you have your grandmother ask him to make you a box with a lid to carry Snowball in."

Mandie frowned. "Put Snowball in a box?" she objected. "Oh, no! I could fix a shallow box for him to sleep in on the train, but I couldn't shut him up in anything."

"That's what I meant," Celia replied. "If you have a box for him on the train, and if it has a lid, you can always keep him from running away. Without it, he could get lost for good on the train or maybe jump off during stops."

Mrs. Taft nodded her approval. "That's a good idea, Celia," she acknowledged. "Amanda, if you insist on carrying him, you've got to have some way to shut him up now and then so you won't lose him when we change trains and all."

Mandie sighed. "The box would have to have lots of air holes in it," she informed them, finally giving in.

"Of course, dear," Mrs. Taft agreed. "I'll mention it to Uncle Ned in the morning. Now, I'm sending a message to Celia's mother in Richmond to ask if we may stay overnight there and go on to the White House the next day. Otherwise, we will be worn out by the time we get to Washington and won't enjoy the visit at all."

"Oh, yes!" Celia squealed with delight. "Then you will get to see our farm and all the horses, Mandie."

"That will be wonderful," Mandie responded excitedly. "I can't wait to get going!"

"I'm not sure how much Mandie will be able to see, Celia," Mrs. Taft countered. "We won't have much time there, and it will probably be dark by the time we arrive. But we'll see."

After the meal, Mandie sat at the desk in the library and wrote a letter to President McKinley while Snowball sat in her lap. The kitten tried to play with the moving pen as Mandie wrote.

When she had finished, Mandie read the letter aloud to her grandmother and Celia for their approval. "Dear President McKinley," she read. "Thank you for inviting me to the White House for your inauguration. My grandmother, Mrs. Norman Taft, and I (and my kitten, Snowball) will arrive in Washington on Friday, March 1, 1901, on the 1:30 train from Richmond, as you requested. Please have someone meet us at the train depot. With love and gratitude, Amanda Elizabeth Shaw." She looked up for their reaction.

Mrs. Taft smiled. "I don't think you have to tell the President of the United States to send someone to meet us, dear," she remarked. "I'm sure he will send his carriage for us."

"Well, we don't want to get lost in that big city up

there," Mandie reminded them. "Besides, we don't want to have to sit in the depot and wait for someone to pick us up."

"We won't have to worry about the President forgetting," Mrs. Taft assured her. "But go ahead and seal it up, dear. I'll get Ben to take it to the post office tomorrow."

Celia sat on the edge of her chair. "Couldn't we take it there today?" she asked.

"No, dear," Mrs. Taft replied. "The post office is not open on Sunday." Then laying her hand on Mandie's, she said, "If you want to send your mother a letter, why don't you get that written too. Then Uncle Ned can take it to her when he comes by in the morning."

"I wish I could see Uncle Ned," Mandie sighed. "But I know we have to go back to school after supper tonight." Turning around, she began writing a quick note to her mother.

"That's right, dear," Mrs. Taft agreed. "Miss Prudence said absolutely no other leave for the rest of the school year.

Mandie handed the note to Mrs. Taft.

Celia's green eyes sparkled. "I don't think Mandie will mind," she said knowingly.

Mandie whirled around in the parlor. "I can't wait to get back to school so I can tell everybody the news," she announced. Celia tightened her lips slightly, but Mandie pretended not to notice.

# *Chapter 7 / The Stranger on the Train*

When the girls got back to school and Mandie looked for someone to tell, there was no one in sight. There was a lamp burning in the office but not a sound of anyone near. She sighed. "All the girls must be in their rooms," she said as they walked toward the stairway.

"Probably," Celia agreed, looking around. "It's almost bedtime." The girls continued on up the stairs.

When they opened the door to their room, they found Aunt Phoebe kneeling before the fireplace, stirring up the logs so that they would give out more warmth. As soon as she saw them she stood up.

Mandie ran to her. "Aunt Phoebe!" she exclaimed. "I'm so glad to see you again. It seems like everybody around here just disappears for days at a time."

"It jes' been necessary lately, Missy," the Negro woman said, wiping her hands on her big white apron.

Mandie hung her coat in the chifferobe, then took Celia's and hung it up.

Celia thanked Mandie and turned back to the old Negro woman. "Guess what, Aunt Phoebe!" she exclaimed excitedly.

"Wait," Mandie said, frowning at her friend. "Let me tell her." Again Mandie ignored the hurt look in Celia's eyes. Grabbing the old woman's hand, she babbled on. "I'm going to Washington to see the President, and you're the very first one here at school to know about it."

Aunt Phoebe straightened up and stared at the girls in surprise. "De real President?" she gasped.

"Yes, ma'am," Mandie replied. "He invited me to the White House because he heard about the hospital we're building for the Cherokee Indians with the gold my friends and I found."

"Lawsy mercy, Missy!" Aunt Phoebe exclaimed. "Come heah and let me touch you. I ain't never heerd such 'citin' news." She reached for Mandie and embraced her. "Goin' to see de real President! Ain't dat somethin'!"

The old Negro woman sat on the rug in front of the fire with the girls as they explained about the forthcoming trip. She listened with her mouth open, and her eyes grew wide with excitement.

When they had finished, Mandie eyed the Negro woman curiously. "Aunt Phoebe, we've told you all our news; now how about telling us what is going on around here with you and Miss Prudence and Miss Hope disappearing every now and then."

Aunt Phoebe struggled to her feet and then straightened her long dress. "I'se real sorry 'bout dat, Missy," she apologized. "But Miz Prudence, she give strict orders dat we ain't s'posed to discuss anythin' wid de school's girls. Now I'se gotta go stir up de fire in my own house. I jes' come to shake this'n up so's y'all git warm when you comes in from de cold tonight." She started toward the door, then looked back.

Mandie stood up and stared at her in dismay. "You

can't even say a single little tiny word?"

"Now, Missy, you knows a promise be's a promise," Aunt Phoebe scolded. "And 'sides, it don't rightly concern you. Now y'all keep on de lookout fo' dat Yankee girl, April. I'll see y'all in de mawnin'. Good night."

"Good night, Aunt Phoebe," the girls chorused as the old woman left the room.

Mandie looked at Celia and smiled. "Guess we won't find out anything unless we do some investigating on our own," she said.

"Which we'd better not do," Celia warned her. "Because if we get in trouble, you know what will happen to your Washington trip."

"Well, we'll just have to keep our eyes and ears open," Mandie told her.

By noon the next day everyone in the school knew about Mandie's invitation to the White House. Mandie felt disappointed that the other students didn't seem impressed by the news. "After all," she kept telling Celia, "it isn't every day that a girl gets invited to meet the President of the United States."

The days passed slowly, but soon Mandie received a reply from her mother, cautioning her to take plenty of warm clothes, to be on her very best behavior, and to mind her grandmother.

As Mandie read the short note, she realized with satisfaction that her mother had not even mentioned the baby brother or sister due in June. Mandie didn't want to think about the baby. That was like a dark cloud hanging over her future happiness.

Although she tried to get over her jealousy, the thought of sharing her mother with another child still made her angry sometimes. Then she would scold herself and try to get her mind on the Washington trip. Whenever she thought about meeting the President of the United States, all other thoughts and worries vanished.

On Saturday, February 23, just a little more than a week before they were to leave, Mandie awoke to find Asheville in the grips of a terrible snowstorm. Before breakfast, as she and Celia sat on a settee in the parlor reading the newspaper, they discovered that there was snow from Charleston, South Carolina, all the way to Texas. LaGrange, Georgia, had ten inches already; Atlanta had five; and Birmingham, Alabama, had six inches. Asheville itself had ten inches, and the weatherman was predicting more snow for the next day.

"Oh, Celia," Mandie moaned, looking up from the paper. "What if it snows so much that we can't get to Washington?"

"But, Mandie, you're going by train," Celia reminded her. "I think trains can get through all kinds of weather. It never has hindered us in Richmond that I can remember. And we have lots more snow at home than Asheville has."

"But it could get worse." Mandie stood and started pacing up and down the wooden parlor floor. "Remember, it snowed six feet of snow in San Francisco, California, on the fourth of January this year, and I don't think that place ever gets much snow."

"Mandie, stop worrying," Celia scolded. "I think God will see that you get there safely. He has helped you this far. I don't think He'll let you down now. You have to trust Him. That's what you've always told me."

Mandie walked back to her friend and sat down again. "You're right," she said, taking Celia's hand. "I think our special verse would help right now, don't you? Because

I'm afraid I won't be able to go. Let's say it together."

Celia joined her as she quoted the Bible verse: "What time I am afraid I will trust in thee."

Then smiling reassuringly at each other, they settled back on the settee and waited for the bell in the backyard to ring for breakfast.

"You know, Celia, I was just thinking," Mandie said after a few minutes. "I don't believe we've heard a single noise in the attic since that night we ignored it. And nothing else has been bothered in our room."

"You're right," Celia replied. "And we haven't seen the mouse anymore, either."

"I just wish we could figure out what has been going on around here with people disappearing for days at a time," Mandie sighed. "The only one who is here every day is Millie, I suppose."

Celia gave her a warning look. "Like Aunt Phoebe said, that doesn't really concern us, so I think we'd better quit worrying about it. If we start poking around and Miss Prudence finds out, we'll both get into trouble."

"Just wait until I get back from Washington. Then we'll see what we can find out," Mandie promised.

---

The snow stopped the next day, and it was all gone by the day of Mandie's departure. Mandie felt silly for all her worrying, but she was so excited about leaving that all else was soon forgotten.

Mandie rushed around "like a chicken with its head cut off," as Aunt Phoebe said, trying to get her packing done in time. Ben was to pick her up on his way to the depot with Mrs. Taft. Celia received permission to go to the station with Aunt Phoebe to see her friend off.

After countless goodbyes, Mandie carried Snowball in the special box Uncle Ned had made and followed her grandmother onto the waiting train. Her eyes filled with tears of joy as she hurried to her seat. Quickly setting the box down, she opened the window and waved to her friends as the cold air rushed in the window.

Aunt Phoebe and Celia stood on the platform with Ben and waved back as the train pulled out of the station. Mandie kept waving until the train rounded a curve and she couldn't see her friends anymore. But for a moment, she just stood there at the open window, staring out into space, hardly able to believe she was finally on her way to see the President.

"Amanda," Mrs. Taft scolded, pulling her fur cape closer about her shoulders. "We're out of sight now, so please close that window before we freeze to death."

Mandie closed the window, then set Snowball's box on her lap and let the kitten out. Setting the box on the floor by her feet, she began petting the soft white kitten in her lap.

Mrs. Taft pulled on her fur cape again. "I don't think the window is closed all the way, dear," she said. "I feel a draft."

As Mandie stood to check the window, Snowball scuttled over into Mrs. Taft's lap, which he had never done before, and curled up in the warm folds of her fur cape.

Mandie struggled with the window, using all her weight to finally get it closed all the way. But before she sat down again, she noticed that a few rows back there was a strange-looking dark-haired man with a small black mustache, staring at her intently. Mandie tried to smile, but there was something about the way he looked at her—

"Amanda, dear," Mrs. Taft interrupted Mandie's thoughts. "Please either take this cat or put him back in his box."

Mandie laughed nervously as she sat down and reached for her white kitten. "Come here, Snowball," she said. "You'd better stay by me. I don't want to have to put you back in the box." Trying to dismiss the sight of the stranger, she turned to her grandmother. "I'm so excited, I'll never be able to sit still," she said.

"You're going to have to sit for a long time, dear, I'm afraid," Mrs. Taft reminded her. "Just relax and watch the scenery go by."

"I'll try, Grandmother," Mandie promised. Curling up in her seat with Snowball in her lap, she pulled her own new fur cape about her. "This cape is so nice and warm I might just go to sleep since I had to get up before daylight this morning. I'm awfully tired from rushing around so much to get ready."

"That's fine, dear," Mrs. Taft replied. "Just relax."

Before long, Mandie lost interest in the trees whizzing past and her eyes began to feel droopy. The next thing Mandie knew, her grandmother was gently shaking her.

"Amanda, dear," Grandmother said, "I just thought you'd like to see where we are."

Mandie blinked her eyes and tried to wake up.

"Look, we're about to cross the state line into Virginia," Grandmother said. "I don't believe you've ever been to Virginia, have you?"

Mandie sat up and rubbed her eyes as Snowball clung to her lap. Glancing back, Mandie felt uneasy. The man with the small black mustache seemed to follow her every move. She shook off the feeling and tried to get her mind on something else.

Pressing her face against the window glass, Mandie could make out a village just coming into sight. Alongside the railroad track, there was a sign that read: Welcome to the Commonwealth of Virginia.

Mandie looked at her grandmother in amazement. "We're actually going into Virginia!" she exclaimed. "You know, I've never been anywhere out of North Carolina, except to Charleston, South Carolina, to visit my friend Tommy's family. Are we almost to Celia's town?"

"Not quite, dear," Mrs. Taft replied. "I'm sure it'll be dark by the time we get to Richmond. But Celia's mother wrote that someone would meet us at the depot."

"Then we'll be leaving early tomorrow morning, won't we?" Mandie asked.

"Yes, dear," Mrs. Taft nodded. "We'll have to get the early train to Washington."

"I won't have time to see much of Celia's farm, then, will I?"

"Probably not," her grandmother agreed. "But there will be other times. . . ."

As the train chugged on, Mandie could sense the man's eyes on her every minute. Who was he?

The sky grew dark, and soon the conductor came through the train, yelling, "Richmond! Next stop, Richmond!"

Mandie felt relieved. She had been aware of the numerous calls for various stops along the way all day, but now her heart beat faster. At last they could get off the train and leave the mysterious man with the mustache behind—she hoped.

Putting Snowball back in his box, Mandie stood with her grandmother, and a redcap came to take their luggage off the train for them.

As they started down the aisle, Mandie turned around to speak to her grandmother. The man with the mustache looked directly at her but did not move. Mandie's heart began to thump. Why did that man keep staring at her? Suddenly she couldn't remember what she had meant to say to her grandmother. She tried desperately to shake off the fear that hung over her.

Stepping off the train onto the depot platform, Mandie clutched Snowball's box tightly and looked around. "So this is Richmond!" She gasped.

People were getting off the train. Redcaps were carrying baggage into the waiting room in the depot. But Mandie could see little else in the darkness, and the train alongside the platform blocked whatever view there was.

"Come on, Amanda," Mrs. Taft called.

The redcap walked ahead of them with their luggage, down the platform toward the waiting room door.

Suddenly a large black woman materialized out of the darkness of the platform, giving Mandie a start. The woman stepped forward to speak to Mrs. Taft. "Y'all must be de people what's 'spected out at de Hamiltons'," she said in a friendly voice.

Mrs. Taft smiled. "Yes, we are," she said. "I'm Mrs. Taft, and this is Miss Amanda."

Mandie took a deep breath, trying to calm herself.

Grandmother spoke again. "Do you have a rig here to take us out to the Hamilton place?"

"Yessum," the Negro woman replied. "My name's May, and me and Abner been waitin' fo' y'all. Abner be in de rig."

Mrs. Taft laid her hand on the woman's arm. "Then stop the redcap with our luggage up there, please, and show him where your rig is," she said.

"Yessum." The woman scurried ahead to catch the redcap, then motioned toward the rig waiting at the end of the platform. The redcap turned and carried the luggage over to the wagon where a small, thin Negro man sat waiting.

Mandie and Mrs. Taft followed.

Abner jumped down from his seat and helped the redcap store the bags in the rig.

May looked at Mrs. Taft. "Y'all jes' git in, Missus," she said.

Mandie jumped inside the closed-in rig and Snowball meowed loudly at the rough treatment. Mandie talked reassuringly to him as Mrs. Taft climbed in and sat beside her granddaughter.

As soon as May and Abner were settled on the seat up front, Abner whipped the horses and got the rig rolling without another word.

Mandie peered into the darkness as they rode through the streets of Richmond, but it was impossible to see much. She sighed. "Oh, I wish I could see everything," she said impatiently. "You know this is not only the capital of Virginia, but it was also the capital of the American Confederacy from 1861 to 1865."

Mrs. Taft patted her hand. "Evidently you have been studying your history," she said.

"And Grandmother, did you know that Thomas Jefferson planned the state capitol building?" Mandie asked.

"Why, yes, I believe I had heard about that." Mrs. Taft sounded amused.

"Just think," Mandie went on. "This time tomorrow, we'll be in the White House! It's so exciting! I can't wait to tell my friends Joe and Sallie all about it . . . and Celia, too, of course," she added.

Staring out into the darkness, her thoughts wandered to the excitement that awaited them.

Celia's mother, Jane Hamilton, and Celia's Aunt Rebecca, whom Mandie had met at the school, welcomed them to their enormous white-columned mansion called Woodlands.

Mandie looked around in awe at the immense house and all the expensive furnishings. But later when she and her grandmother said good night in the hallway upstairs, Mandie confided, "It's all beautiful and huge and everything, but I don't believe it measures up to your house, Grandmother."

Mrs. Taft spoke in soft tones. "Well, your grandfather had a little more money than the Hamiltons," she said proudly. "And he felt the best place to spend part of it was on a home that could be passed down from one generation to another."

"This house is almost a museum, I think," Mandie said in awe.

"Well, just relax and enjoy your brief stay, dear," her grandmother replied. "We must be getting to bed. We have to get up early to catch the train to Washington, and we want to be well rested." She bent to kiss Mandie's forehead. "Good night, dear," she said.

Mandie gave her a big hug. "Good night, Grandmother. I hope I can sleep tonight, but I don't think I'll really be able to relax until this trip is over and I'm back home again."

"Well, at least try," Mrs. Taft urged, heading down the hallway to the room she was to occupy.

After Mandie went to bed, she tossed and turned, excited about the next day, but also bothered about the mysterious man on the train. *At least he didn't follow us off the train*, she thought. Finally she fell into a fitful sleep, dreaming about trains and mansions and men with mustaches.

When the Hamiltons' maid woke her before dawn the next morning, she quickly jumped out of bed, looking forward to the exciting day ahead.

After a quick breakfast, May and Abner drove Mandie and her grandmother and Snowball to the train depot. The excited travelers were soon on their way.

But as Mandie looked curiously around the train car, she caught her breath. There, two rows back on the other side of the train sat the man with the small black mustache. His dark eyes bore into her, and he did not smile. Mandie's heart pounded louder and louder in her ears. What was *he* doing here? Was this man following them? And more importantly, why?

Oh, how Mandie wished her grandmother had not insisted that they wear their fur capes on the train! Maybe the man intended to rob them! Mandie cringed, knowing that Grandmother had brought her expensive jewelry to wear to the Inaugural Ball.

Mandie turned around and stared straight ahead, but her heart pounded. She couldn't get her mind off the man with the small black mustache.

## *Chapter 8 / Meet the President*

As Mandie started to get off the train in the nation's capital, she glanced back. The man with the mustache stood and buttoned his suit coat. Mandie felt hot all over and her heart beat wildly. She had decided against telling her grandmother about the man, but now she wished she had.

Clutching Snowball's box, she made her feet move forward. As she stood ready to step off the train, she hardly had time to look around at the elaborate train station.

There, on the platform directly in front of Mandie, stood a tall, well-dressed man whom she recognized immediately. He had brought the President's invitation to Mandie at her mother and Uncle John's home in Franklin, North Carolina. She heaved a sigh of relief. No matter who that stranger on the train was, they were safe now with the President's man in Washington, D.C. The man held out his hand and helped Mandie down the high train steps.

Snowball meowed softly. Mandie ignored Snowball's protest and put on her best social graces, the way Miss

Prudence taught her students to do. "Thank you, Mr. . . . Mr. . . . why, I don't believe I know your name, sir. But I know you work for President McKinley."

"Adam Adamson, at your service, Miss Amanda," the man replied.

Mandie stepped aside as the man helped Mrs. Taft down the train steps.

Mandie's grandmother carefully stepped onto the platform. "Thank you so much, Mr. Adamson," she said quite properly. "It was so nice of you to come and meet us."

Mr. Adamson bowed slightly, tipping his hat. "I'm the President's personal assistant, madam," he said, "and though I am delighted to see you and Miss Amanda again, I must admit that it is simply part of my job to see that you are taken directly to the White House."

"You don't know how glad I am to see you," Mandie told him. Just then her white kitten meowed again, this time more loudly. "Snowball, please behave," she scolded, tapping his box lightly. Then she turned her attention to Mr. Adamson again. "Is President McKinley at home?" she asked eagerly.

"Yes, he's at home," Mr. Adamson replied. "However, you know his office is in the White House, so he does his work there," he explained. "Right this way, ladies." He led the way up some stairs and out onto the street.

Mandie's eyes grew wide as she saw a beautiful coach with four white horses waiting for them. A wiry Negro man on the high front seat quickly jumped down and opened the coach door. Mandie noticed the presidential seal on the door. The driver bowed slightly and smiled.

"Here we are," Mr. Adamson said, assisting Mrs. Taft and then Mandie into the coach. He climbed in after them, and they went on their way through the streets of Washington.

Mandie held Snowball's box on her lap, but she could hardly sit still. With no more thought of the stranger on the train, Mandie thrilled as Mr. Adamson pointed out various landmarks on their way.

"That is the Capitol building," Mr. Adamson pointed out.

Peering through the window, Mandie recognized the huge white building with many columns and a high dome from pictures she had seen at school. "The Capitol!" she exclaimed. "It's enormous. And it looks so tall."

"It is rather large," the man agreed. "It takes a lot of people to run such a big country.

Mandie kept her face glued to the window as they traveled on. Soon another enormous building came into sight. "What is that great big building there?" she asked.

"That is the State, War, and Navy building, Miss Amanda," Mr. Adamson told her. Then he began explaining what the function of the Department of State was.

Mandie interrupted him to show off her knowledge, and he was surprised.

"Amanda, dear, please let Mr. Adamson continue with his explanation," Mrs. Taft said softly.

Mandie turned to apologize. "I'm sorry, Mr. Adamson. I'm just so excited, 'I'm bustin' at the seams,' as our cook, Aunt Lou, would say."

"I understand," Mr. Adamson replied. "That's perfectly all right. Just don't bust your seams before you get a chance to meet the President," he added with a grin.

They all laughed.

In a few minutes they rode up the curved cobblestone driveway to the front of the White House. Mandie sat speechless as she gazed at the big white mansion with ten enormous columns holding up the roof to the front porch.

She reached for Mrs. Taft's hand and squeezed hard. "I'm afraid I'm dreaming and I'll wake up any minute," she said.

Mrs. Taft smiled down at her. "I know I'm not dreaming, and I don't believe you are either, dear," she responded as the coach came to a halt by the front steps.

The driver quickly opened the door of the coach, and Mr. Adamson stepped out to assist Mrs. Taft and Mandie. Snowball mewed loudly from inside his box, apparently not liking the shaking he got as his mistress left the coach. Mandie spoke comfortingly to him, then turned her attention back to their host.

Mr. Adamson led the way up the front steps to the White House. "I have been instructed to take you directly to the President's personal quarters where you will meet the First Lady," he explained. "Then you will be given a room to rest in until the President finishes his day's work and can join you for supper."

A uniformed butler, standing just inside the front doorway, quickly pushed the door open as they walked across the front porch.

Suddenly Mrs. Taft stopped in her tracks. "My word!" she exclaimed. "I was so distracted, I didn't even remember our baggage on the train! Oh, dear!"

Mr. Adamson smiled. "Your baggage will probably be in your rooms by the time you get there," he said. "You see, the driver had someone get it off the train while you and Miss Amanda were talking to me at the station."

Mrs. Taft looked embarrassed. "How could I have been so addled?"

Mandie gripped Snowball's box tighter. "They sure must have been fast," she said. "But how did they know which baggage belonged to us?"

Mr. Adamson turned to her. "You didn't know this, but the President sent an agent to ride the train to Washington with you," he explained, "just to make sure you arrived safely. He rode in the same car with you."

Mandie's eyes grew wide. "Did this man by any chance have a small black mustache?" she asked, suddenly remembering the man who wouldn't take his eyes off her.

Mr. Adamson smiled. "Why, yes," he replied. "That was our man, Tadford."

Instantly Mandie felt relieved and honored. The President had cared enough to send a man just to make sure that nothing happened to them on the train. She shook her head at how fast she had jumped to the wrong conclusions.

Mr. Adamson held the door and waited for the ladies to go through the doorway. "Don't forget," he cautioned, "you are the guests of the President of the United States."

Mandie held her head high. Hardly noticing the maid who took their wraps, she gazed about in wonder at the magnificence of the White House furnishings in the entrance hall. This was *the* White House, and she was inside it, standing on her own two feet. And she would soon meet the President himself. It was *not* a dream. Her heart beat rapidly as she continued to look around, and soon she became so weak-kneed that she wasn't sure she could take another step.

Then her grandmother's hand on her arm broke the spell. "Amanda, we are waiting," Mrs. Taft said, smiling.

"I'm sorry," Mandie quickly replied. "I'm just scared to death."

"But you have nothing to be afraid of, Miss Amanda," Mr. Adamson encouraged as he led the way down the hallway.

"Oh, but I do!" Mandie cried, trying to keep up with his long strides. "You see, I'm always getting into trouble doing things I shouldn't. I'm so afraid I'll do something wrong while I'm in the White House."

Mr. Adamson shook his head slowly in amusement. "I don't think you have anything to worry about," he responded. "You see, the President loves young people. He had two little daughters of his own but lost both of them when they were small. Ever since then, he has been lonely for children."

"I'm so sorry," Mandie murmured sadly. "I guess I never thought about whether the President had any children or not."

"I'm confident he will greatly enjoy your visit," Mr. Adamson assured her.

After getting permission to take Snowball from his box, Mandie left the box with a servant and clutched her kitten tightly as they made their way down the hallway to the President's quarters. Mandie noticed many men and women in uniforms—maids and butlers—she couldn't possibly guess what they each did. And the hallways seemed miles long.

Finally Mr. Adamson came to a stop outside an ornate door. "This is the President's parlor, where the First Lady is waiting to receive you," he told them.

Mrs. Taft threw back her shoulders and straightened her dress. Mandie held her breath and waited for him to open the door.

Pushing the door inward, Mr. Adamson cleared his throat. "Mrs. Norman Taft and Miss Amanda Shaw, Mrs. McKinley," he announced.

Mandie gasped at the lavish room. Mr. Adamson stepped aside and allowed them to enter, then left the room, closing the door behind him.

A beautiful, woman with wavy, graying auburn hair, which she wore parted in the middle, rose from a seat near the glowing fire in the fireplace. Her lavender silk gown set off her fair skin. "Welcome, Mrs. Taft and Miss Shaw," she said. Smiling, Mrs. McKinley continued, "The President and I are so happy you could come for a visit. Won't you please sit down?" The President's wife pointed them to a settee across from her and she sat back down.

"Thank you, Mrs. McKinley," Mrs. Taft replied, taking a place on the settee. "It is a great honor to meet you."

Mandie held Snowball tightly. "Yes, thank you, Mrs. McKinley," she said with a quaver in her voice. "I . . . I'm so excited I just can't think of anything else to say. Please forgive me." She hurried to sit beside her grandmother.

"I know how you feel, dear," the First Lady said kindly. "When I was your age, I never dreamed I would ever meet the President of the United States. And here I am *married* to him." She gave a little laugh.

Just then a trim maid in a neat uniform hurried in with a tea cart and wheeled it over to Mrs. McKinley. Taking the teapot and china from the cart, she placed it on the table between the two settees. Mandie was glad to see that there were several plates of gooey-looking sweet treats.

Suddenly Snowball squirmed and leaped out of Mandie's grasp onto the floor. Mandie quickly jumped up and snatched at him as he hurried to the hearth by the warm fire.

"Snowball, come back here!" Mandie scolded, reaching for him.

Mrs. McKinley didn't seem disturbed at all. "Let him stay there, dear," she said as she began pouring the tea. "Do you think he would drink some milk?"

"Oh, sure," Mandie said, sitting down again. "He'll eat anything you give him."

Mrs. McKinley turned to the maid, who stood by the cart. "Antoinette, would you please take a saucer and pour some milk in it?" she asked. "Then just put it on the hearth there for the kitten."

"Yes, madam," Antoinette replied. Mandie detected a foreign accent and decided it was French because of her name.

Antoinette immediately made friends with Snowball and kept filling the saucer with milk as he drank it. Mandie watched out of the corner of her eye as the maid softly encouraged the cat to drink more. Mandie could only faintly hear what she was saying, but it didn't sound like English. Amused, she wondered if Snowball could understand French.

Before long, as they all sipped tea and nibbled on sweet cakes, Mandie's grandmother and Mrs. McKinley were carrying on a conversation as though they were old friends. The First Lady was so warm, friendly, and down-to-earth that Mandie liked her at once.

Mandie wasn't sure how they got on the subject of dishes, but Mrs. McKinley was telling Mrs. Taft about the presidential china that President Harrison's wife had started collecting. "I have made that my project, as well, to continue working on the collection," she said. She had Antoinette show Mrs. Taft the fancy white and gold punch bowl on a pedestal that had been used during the Franklin Pierce administration.

As they finished tea, Mrs. McKinley said, "Antoinette

will show you to your rooms so you can rest and freshen up before supper. She has a daughter, Isabelle, who will be your maid while you are here.

"Thank you," Mrs. Taft replied, rising from the settee. "We look forward to dining with you and the President later."

Mandie hurriedly snatched up Snowball. "Yes, thank you, Mrs. McKinley," she responded. "I was really hungry and thirsty after that long train ride. And so was Snowball."

"I thought you might be, dear," the First Lady replied. "Have a nice rest now, and we'll see you at supper."

After following Antoinette through a maze of hallways, they finally stopped outside a room. Antoinette threw the door open. Inside, a dark-haired girl in a uniform was fluffing pillows and straightening the bedspread.

Antoinette turned to Mrs. Taft. "Madam, your room," she said, motioning her inside. Then quickly walking across the hallway, she opened another door and said to Mandie, "Mademoiselle, your boudoir. Isabelle will attend you also." Before Mandie could even say thank you, Antoinette hurried off down the hallway.

Instead of going into her own room, Mandie crossed the hall to her grandmother's, where the door was still open. She went inside. To her amazement, her grandmother was carrying on a rapid conversation in French with the young maid Isabelle. She had no idea her grandmother could speak any language other than English.

Suddenly Mrs. Taft turned to Mandie and said something in French.

Mandie gasped. "Grandmother, I can't understand a word you're saying."

"Amanda, do you mean Miss Prudence has not been

teaching you French?" she demanded in exasperation.

"No, Grandmother," Mandie replied, holding her squirming kitten tightly. "No one has even mentioned it to me."

"Well, there must be some misunderstanding," Mrs. Taft said, shaking her head. "That was one reason your mother selected Miss Prudence's school. She wanted you to learn French and music and all the social graces."

"I know Miss Prudence has a French class for some of the girls, but no one told me I was supposed to take it," Mandie protested. "I'm not sure I could learn to speak another language."

"Oh, but you will, Amanda," her grandmother assured her. "It is absolutely necessary. Remember, when we go to Europe, there is very little English spoken over there—except in England, of course."

"That's one time you'll just have to do all the talking," Mandie teased. "But I didn't even know you could speak French until just now."

"I've never had the occasion to use it around you, I suppose," Mrs. Taft replied. "However, people say I am very good at it—speaking or reading."

Snowball kept squirming, trying to get down. In his furious attempt to get free, he scratched Mandie.

"Ow!" Mandie cried. "Grandmother, would you please ask that girl if she knows how we can get a sandbox for Snowball? I think that's what he needs right now."

To Mandie's surprise, Isabelle smiled and said in English, "Come with me, Miss Amanda. We are prepared for Snowball." Leading the way back across the hallway to Mandie's room, she walked over to a fancy mahogany box in one corner and pointed. "Snowball's bathroom," she said.

Seeing the box full of sand, Mandie let the kitten jump down into it and turned back to the girl. "Thank you, Isabelle. It was nice of you to have that ready for him."

"Oh, but Miss Amanda, it was not I who thought of this," Isabelle said quickly. "It was the President himself. He said, 'Isabelle, Miss Amanda says in her letter she is bringing Snowball, her kitten. Therefore, we must have something prepared for him, too.' " She gestured as she talked. "So he had the box full of sand put there, just for Snowball. He says we should not let the kitten out of the house, also. Snowball could get lost."

"Oh, the President must be such a nice man. I'm so eager to meet him!" Mandie exclaimed, glancing around the room full of beautiful furnishings. "And I just love this house!"

Isabelle agreed and then left Mandie by herself to rest. It seemed she had just drifted off to sleep when Isabelle knocked on the doors to tell Mandie and her grandmother they had one hour to get dressed for dinner. Then they were to meet the President in his parlor.

Mandie got up quickly and found that not only had her bags been taken to her room, but someone had unpacked them and put her things in the bureau and wardrobe.

Mandie kept trying on the new dresses her grandmother had bought for her, unable to decide just what to wear. After helping Mrs. Taft, Isabelle came into Mandie's room.

"Which one, Isabelle?" Mandie asked.

"The blue one, to match your eyes." The maid pointed to the pale blue silk.

"Thanks," Mandie said, holding up the dress. "That's the one I had just about decided on, anyway. Do you think it will be suitable—I mean, the way it's made?"

"Very appropriate," Isabelle smiled. "High neck, long sleeves, so you don't have to wear a shawl. It gets drafty in the dining room sometimes. Here. Let me help."

With Isabelle's assistance, Mandie got the blue silk dress on over the necessary petticoats, then turned to the mirror to decide what to do with her long blonde hair.

Isabelle pulled Mandie's hair back, leaving a few loose ends over Mandie's ears. "Like this," she said. "Tie a blue ribbon right here."

Mandie quickly got a blue ribbon from the bureau drawer. Isabelle threaded the ribbon through Mandie's hair and tied it in a big bow.

"That looks nice," Mandie said, admiring herself in the mirror. "I'll have to get you to show me how to do that."

"You need some jewelry," Isabelle decided.

Mandie reached into her jewelry box and chose the sand dollar on a chain that Tommy had given her for Christmas.

Isabelle approved and helped her fasten it.

Mandie twirled around and around before the mirror. The elegant floor-length blue silk dress made Mandie feel grown up. Actually, the dress was a little too long and covered her feet, but that didn't bother Mandie. She was happy.

The clock on the mantel struck five.

"It is time, Miss Amanda," Isabelle announced. "Let's get your grandmother and go to the parlor."

Mandie's legs would hardly carry her down the hallways as she and her grandmother followed Isabelle to the President's parlor.

Isabelle paused at the door, tapping lightly before

opening it. Then, as the young maid pushed the door open, Mandie saw a tall, portly man with brown hair and a cleft chin. He was standing before the fireplace. Her heart beat wildly. *The President!*

Mandie's heart pounded as Isabelle announced the guests. "Mrs. Norman Taft and Miss Amanda Shaw, Mr. President." She led them through the doorway. "Is there anything else, sir?"

The President dismissed the maid and turned to smile at Mandie. "Ah, Miss Amanda Shaw," he said warmly. "Do come in and sit down. It is such a great pleasure to make your acquaintance."

Mandie couldn't move. Mrs. Taft had to take her hand and lead her into the room. Mrs. McKinley motioned to a settee where they sat down.

Later, Mandie could hardly remember what went on in that room. The President centered most of his attention on Mandie while his wife entertained Mrs. Taft until dinner was announced. Mandie knew that she and the President had carried on a conversation about the hospital for the Cherokees, but as she lay in the big bed in the guest room that night with Snowball curled up on the other pillow, all she could remember was her embarrassment.

As soon as she had sat on the settee, her dress moved slightly upward and she glanced down to see that she was still wearing her *bedroom slippers*! Her face felt as if it were on fire, and as she tried to hold her feet backward under her dress, hoping the President wouldn't notice, she couldn't concentrate on a thing the man was saying. The whole time, she kept watching, hoping he wouldn't look down at her feet.

Even when they went into the dining room and her feet were well hidden under the table, Mandie was still so

uncomfortable she could hardly eat a bite.

She was relieved when everybody said good night and went to their rooms. Fortunately, her grandmother had never noticed the bedroom slippers. She wasn't sure whether the President had or not.

## *Chapter 9 / Footsteps in the Hall*

As Mandie lay in bed, staring at the crackling fire in the fireplace, she relived the evening over and over again. She was so lost in thought that she didn't hear the noise in the hallway at first. Then it seemed to grow louder, and she sat up to listen.

*It must be awfully late*, she thought, but it sounded like someone shuffling down the hallway. She was sure she heard the footsteps go down the hallway and back up twice.

Finally Mandie got up enough nerve to creep over to the door, and open it a crack. The White House was spooky after dark, with so many hallways and rooms—even though it was lit here and there.

At first she couldn't see anyone, but then as she started to close the door, a figure came shuffling down the hallway toward her room. Holding the door open only far enough to peek through the crack with one eye, she gasped in disbelief as the figure passed her room. *It couldn't be him!* she thought, her heart pounding. *He's dead! Long years ago!*

Quickly closing the door, she caught her breath, then

jerked the door open again and looked out. There was no one in sight. Glancing up and down the hallway a moment she thought, *Did I just imagine that? Or am I completely losing my senses?*

Mandie closed the door and made sure it was tightly shut. Then she ran and jumped back into bed and covered up with the warm quilts. *Snowball hasn't even moved,* she thought. *If he didn't hear anything, maybe my imagination is just running away with me.*

Oh, how she wished Celia were here to talk to. And oh, how she wished for daylight to come.

Exhausted from her long journey, Mandie slept so soundly that she didn't hear the soft knock on her door the next morning. She awakened to the gentle shaking of her shoulder.

"Mandie," a familiar voice whispered.

Mandie awoke with a start. Quickly she sat up in bed to see her friend, Sallie Sweetwater, Uncle Ned's granddaughter, smiling down at her. Mandie rubbed her eyes and blinked. "Sallie? Are you really here or am I dreaming?" she asked in confusion. "How did you get here?"

Sallie laughed. "The President sent for me to come visit, too," she said.

Snowball lifted his head off the pillow where he was sleeping, then went back to sleep.

Mandie swung her feet onto the carpet and stretched. "Oh, Sallie, this is too good to be true! Yesterday when we were driving through Washington, looking at all the sights, I wished you were here to see everything with me." She rubbed her eyes again. Then seeing the door open a crack, she reached for her robe and slipped into it. "Are you sure I'm not dreaming?"

Suddenly Mandie heard a voice from the hallway. "I

don't think you're dreaming," it said.

Mandie caught her breath. "Joe!" she exclaimed, instantly recognizing the voice of her long-time friend, Joe Woodard. He was two years older than Mandie, and she had grown up with him in Charley Gap before moving to Franklin.

Pulling her robe tightly about her, she ran to peek into the hallway. "Joe, I'm so glad to see you," she said breathlessly. "You can't imagine what happened to me last night! Just wait out there a minute until I get dressed."

She closed the door, then rushed about the room, finding clothes and getting dressed while she babbled with Sallie. "Nobody told me you and Joe were coming here," she said, slipping into a new pink dress.

Sallie perched on the arm of a chair nearby. "I did not know either until three days ago," she replied. "Then someone brought my grandfather the message that he was to bring Joe and me to the White House. I could not believe it. I knew you were going because my grandfather had told me, but I did not know Joe and I were being invited, also."

As Mandie finished buttoning her dress, she noticed with surprise that her friend was fashionably attired in a pretty red silk dress. Sallie always wore skirts, waists, and moccasins—Indian fashion. "You look absolutely beautiful, Sallie!" Mandie exclaimed. "I've never seen you so dressed up."

Sallie stood up, straightened her full skirt and smiled. "It may be beautiful, but it is not comfortable," she replied. "Do you know who got me all dressed up?"

Mandie shook her head.

"Your mother," Sallie replied.

"I might have known," Mandie said, pulling on her

stockings. "But how? You live so far away from my mother."

"The man from the President's office found my grandfather at your house. Then your mother had my grandfather rush home to bring Joe and me there," she explained. "You should see Joe in his fine clothes."

"I imagine he's fussing about them, too," Mandie replied. "I don't like all this finery either, but Grandmother bought all these things for me." She paused for a moment, thinking. "Did you bring your regular clothes with you?" she asked. "I slipped one of my school dresses into my valise without Grandmother knowing about it."

"I also brought comfortable clothes, so I could at least wear them on the journey home," Sallie told her.

"Let's put them on," Mandie said, quickly reaching for her buttons.

"No, Mandie, we cannot do that right now," Sallie told her. "Joe and I are waiting to meet the President and the First Lady. We got here early before they were up and dressed, so we will have breakfast with them and you and your grandmother."

Mandie sighed. "I suppose we'd better wear all these fine clothes until you and Joe meet the President," she said. "Then when he gets busy, we'll change first chance we get." She quickly brushed out her long hair. "Where is your room?" she asked.

"I am to share this one with you," Sallie replied. "Joe is sharing a room with my grandfather, and they are next to your grandmother's room."

"Uncle Ned is staying here too! Oh, that's great, Sallie!" Mandie exclaimed. "But where is your luggage?"

"Outside in the hallway," Sallie answered.

Mandie quickly tied a pink ribbon in her hair, then

hurried to the door and opened it. Joe had propped his lanky frame against the opposite wall, and there he stood, waiting. As the girls stepped into the hallway, Joe picked up Sallie's bag and set it inside Mandie's room. Then closing the door carefully so Snowball wouldn't get out, he rejoined the girls in the hallway.

"Oh, Joe!" Mandie said excitedly, "I'm so glad you and Sallie were invited. And Sallie says Uncle Ned is here, too."

Joe smiled and nodded, running his long, bony fingers through his unruly brown hair.

Mandie looked him over from head to toe. "You really look nice in all those Sunday-go-to-meeting clothes," she said with a giggle.

Joe looked a little embarrassed. "Well, your dress is even fancier than Sunday-go-to-meeting clothes." He laughed. "But Uncle Ned just wore his deerskin jacket and pants and moccasins, like usual."

"I'm glad he is just his old self in the White House," Mandie replied. "He doesn't have to pretend to be anything else."

Joe looked around in the hallway. "Isn't this exciting, being here?" he said, looking around in awe. "It's so much larger than I ever imagined. We could get lost in it."

"We sure could," Mandie agreed. She huddled closer to her friends. "Wait till you hear what happened last night," she told them. "I was trying to go to sleep all by myself in that spooky room, and I kept hearing someone scuffing their shoes as they walked up and down the hallway."

Joe and Sallie looked at each other skeptically.

Mandie continued. "I finally got up enough nerve to look out," she said. "And do you know what I saw? I saw

George Washington walking down the hall."

Joe howled with laughter. "What a tale! It couldn't possibly have been George Washington," he protested. "He's been dead over a hundred years."

"I know that, but I still say I saw him. He looked just like the pictures I've always seen," Mandie insisted. "Now, Joe Woodard, don't you go spoiling things. I intend to find out exactly what was going on last night."

Joe looked exasperated. "Mandie, this is the White House," he warned. "You can't go poking around in it like you do at school or at home when you get involved in some mysterious adventure. You'll get into trouble if you start messing in something that doesn't concern you."

"Look, Joe Woodard." Mandie faced him defiantly. "If I want to investigate, you can't stop me."

Joe straightened his thin shoulders. "I know I can't stop you," he admitted, "but I also will not help you."

Mandie looked up into his brown eyes. "I won't be needing your help, thank you." She spoke a bit more sharply than she had intended.

Sallie shot her a look of concern.

Hearing someone coming down the long hallway, Mandie and her friends turned to see Antoinette approaching them. They greeted her as she got closer.

"Good morning," the maid replied in her French accent. "It is time for breakfast. I have come for Isabelle. Is she with Mrs. Taft?"

Mandie walked across the hall to her grandmother's room. "I don't know, Antoinette. I haven't been in there this morning," she said, tapping lightly on the door. She pushed it open. There was Isabelle, putting the finishing touches on Mrs. Taft's thick, faded blonde hair.

Antoinette leaned into the room. "Isabelle, breakfast

is about to be served," she told her. "We must go now, Madam Taft."

Mandie's grandmother looked up and smiled.

Sallie looked at Joe and asked. "Do you know where my grandfather is?"

"Oh, he left our room awhile ago," Joe replied. "He said he was going to look around before breakfast."

"Please come now, so I can show you the way," Antoinette said, leading them down the long hallway.

A few minutes later they entered the President's parlor. Antoinette announced each guest.

The President, standing by the fire, turned to greet them. But Mandie's attention quickly turned to Uncle Ned, who was gazing out the window. She whispered to Sallie, "Your grandfather has already been talking with the President."

"Yes," Sallie replied softly.

As everyone except Uncle Ned sat down, Mrs. Taft turned to Mandie. "I think it was wonderful of President McKinley to invite your friends, too," she whispered.

Mandie suddenly realized that her grandmother had not seemed surprised when she saw Sallie and Joe with her in the hallway. "Did you know they were coming?" she asked quietly.

"No, but I was taking a walk when they came in," Grandmother Taft explained in a whisper. "I've been awake for hours, it seems."

Mandie looked up as the President began to speak. "You know, if all young people were like you three, we would have no need to fear the future," he said kindly. "I know you are part Cherokee, Miss Amanda. However, you live in the white world, and I think you must have a great deal of compassion if you were willing to use the gold you found to build a hospital for the Indians."

He stood and strolled over by the fireplace again. "The Lord made us all, you know," he said. "And we should treat everyone as our brother or sister because we are all His children. But I'm afraid there are many people who put themselves first and never care about another's misery."

Uncle Ned turned from the window, but just stood there listening.

"And you, Miss Sallie," the President continued, "you are such a shining example for your people. I sincerely hope that you will continue your education and will perhaps someday be in a position to help your fellow Cherokees." The President walked back to the group and laid his hand on Joe's shoulder. "Young man," he said, "I understand your father is a wonderful doctor. I hope you follow in his footsteps."

Joe looked up into the President's face. "No, sir, I don't intend to be a doctor. I want to practice law," he replied honestly.

The President smiled and raised one bushy eyebrow. "An attorney, no less." He seemed pleased.

"Yes, sir, like you," Joe said with a grin.

"Then perhaps one day you will also enter politics and eventually become a resident of this house," he responded. "I wish you well and hope I live to see it, son."

Mandie watched for Joe's reaction.

"Thank you, sir." Joe looked at him directly. "But I'm not aiming that high. I'd like to practice law in my own part of the country—be a country lawyer, like my father is a country doctor."

"I think that would be very gratifying," the President agreed. Turning to Mrs. Taft, he said, "I believe your husband was a senator, wasn't he, Mrs. Taft?"

"Yes, Mr. President," she replied sadly. "In a way. You see, he was elected by the people, but he passed away before he was sworn in," she explained. "God rest his soul."

Mandie was surprised. She had no idea her grandfather was a politician. All she knew was that he had been dead for years. But in spite of how long it had been, she noticed that her grandmother's eyes still glistened with tears.

The President looked down quickly. "Oh, dear. I'm so sorry," he apologized. "I didn't know all the details, I can assure you."

Mandie was glad when Antoinette came back into the room to announce breakfast, but Mrs. Taft looked around curiously. "Is Mrs. McKinley not joining us?" she asked.

"No, I'm afraid she is under the weather this morning," the President replied. "You see, she is not strong. Her health is forever giving her problems. But if you folks will just follow Antoinette, she'll take us to the dining room." He turned to Uncle Ned. "Let's go get a bite to eat, Mr. Sweetwater," he said.

Mandie looked up. That was the first time she had ever heard the old Indian called by his last name. He was just Uncle Ned to everyone. The Indian smiled at her and followed the others into the hallway.

The President turned to Mandie. "Then after breakfast I have a surprise for you young people," he announced.

## *Chapter 10 / Voices in a Locked Room*

As soon as breakfast was over, Mandie found out what the President's surprise was. He had important business to attend to, so he turned his guests over to Mr. Adamson for a sightseeing tour.

At first Mandie didn't think this was much of a surprise, but when the President's coach took them to the Washington Monument, Mandie squealed with delight. "Oh, I was hoping we would get to visit this."

She craned her neck to look out of the carriage at the tall, white, shaft-like marble and granite structure with a pyramid-shaped top. For a moment she felt goosebumps on her arm as she thought about the man she had seen in the hall the night before. This was a monument to George Washington!

Joe let out a low whistle. "That thing almost looks like a giant white pencil," he said, "—if you colored the tip black."

Mandie ignored his attempt to be funny. "We learned about this at school. Could we go inside it?" she asked.

Mr. Adamson helped them out of the carriage. "Of course, Miss Amanda," he said. "In fact, there are 898 steps up to the top, and if you think you can make it, you can climb up all the way to the observation area there." He pointed up. "The view is breathtaking!"

They all looked up and Mandie noticed some tiny-looking windows in the pyramid part.

Sallie grabbed Mandie's arm. "All the way up there?" she asked.

Mandie smiled. "Come on, Sallie. It'll be fun. Let's all go," she urged.

"I'm ready," Joe told her.

"Ned go with Papoose and friends," the old Indian offered.

Mandie's grandmother laughed. "Not me."

"That's all right, ma'am," Mr. Adamson said. "I'll stay here with you."

"Let's go," Mandie urged, starting to run.

"Just a minute." Mr. Adamson stopped her. "There's one more thing you might want to pay attention to inside."

"What's that, sir?" Joe asked.

"Well, one way the government financed the building of this great monument to our first president was to ask people to contribute some of the stones used in the construction," he explained. "So there are 190 carved tribute blocks along the stairway donated by various states and territories, cities and foreign countries, groups and individuals. Watch for those and see where they came from. I know there's one from North Carolina, your home state. See if you can find it."

"That sounds great!" Mandie said excitedly. "Let's go." She turned to her grandmother. "We'll wave to you from the top," she teased.

"That's just fine," Mrs. Taft replied, "but I don't think we'll be able to see you."

Mandie laughed and the young people were off with Uncle Ned walking briskly to keep up with them.

Inside the monument, Mandie wished she had dressed more warmly. The interior was cold and damp, and not very well lit. She pulled her wraps around her and shivered as they started up the stairs. "Let's count the steps on the way up and then look for the carved blocks on the way back down," she said, beginning to count as she climbed. "One, two, three . . ."

"Good idea," Joe answered.

Sallie grabbed Mandie's hand as she climbed beside her friend.

The young people hurried at first, then began to pant and slow down long before Mandie thought they would have to.

When they reached step number 562, Mandie stopped to catch her breath. "I don't know if I can make it all the way to the top," she complained. "My legs hurt."

"Papoose can make it," Uncle Ned encouraged, panting. "Ned not quit. Papoose not quit either. Just take slow. This not race."

Joe and Sallie nodded in agreement, and all four of them stood there for a few minutes, resting before going on again very slowly.

Although there were several more times when Mandie thought she couldn't make it, Uncle Ned and Joe kept urging her and Sallie on until at last Mandie counted off "894—" She was really huffing and puffing now. "—895 . . . 896 . . . 897 . . ." She placed her foot on the top step. "898!" she cried. "We did it!" Perspiring and exhausted, she hugged Sallie. "Let's look out of the windows now," she suggested, her excitement overcoming her fatigue.

Other people milling around in the observation area

glanced at Mandie and smiled.

Mandie led the way to the windows and looked down. "Oh, my goodness!" she cried. "Look how far down it is from here." She swayed slightly, feeling a little light-headed.

"But isn't it beautiful?" Sallie said, apparently glad she had consented to make the climb. "What is that river down there?"

"That's the Potomac—if I remember correctly from my geography lessons," Joe replied.

"You're right, Joe," Mandie agreed. "I just can't believe how small everything seems. That's a pretty big river, and it looks like a satin hair ribbon from up here. And look! I think that's Grandmother and Mr. Adamson down there in front, isn't it?" She laughed. "They look like little ants on the walkway, don't they?" She waved and called to them even though she knew they couldn't see or hear from that far away.

For quite awhile, Uncle Ned and the young people enjoyed the view, pointing out landmarks like the capitol building and the White House to each other. Then, having caught their breath, they finally began their descent. Now they watched for the inscribed blocks Mr. Adamson had told them about. Mandie had seen some of them on the way up, but she didn't want to take the time to stop and read the inscription.

They didn't count how many they saw, but Mandie did try to memorize some of them so she could tell her grandmother and everyone else back home. They found one from the country of Greece, one from China, others from Japan, Switzerland, Turkey, and many other countries. One stone said it had been brought by an American from the historic library in Alexandria, Egypt! They even found some stones donated by Sunday schools and fire departments. Many of the stones were carved with inscriptions about the states that donated them.

"This one is all the way from California," Mandie told the others. "It calls itself the 'youngest sister of the Union.' "

"Look . . . this one," Uncle Ned said, stopping to examine it more closely. "This stone has carving of whale."

"Let me see," Joe urged, crowding the old Indian. "It says it is from New Bedford, and the date is 1851. I suppose it has a whale on it because New Bedford is one of those whaling ports in Massachusetts."

Uncle Ned nodded thoughtfully as they continued on.

Sallie was the one who found the North Carolina stone. "It mentions the state's Mecklenburg Declaration of Independence in May 1775," she told them, her dark eyes sparkling. "We learned about this in history class."

Some time later Mandie let out a squeal. "Oh, come here!" she cried. "Look, Uncle Ned! Look, Sallie! This stone was given by the Cherokees!" She swallowed hard and felt tears coming to her eyes.

"Ned proud, Papoose," the old Indian replied.

"I did not know anything about this," Sallie said.

"Ned remember something about stone for Father of Country, but not know this what for!" He gestured, indicating the tall monument they were in.

"That's really great, Mandie," Joe said. "You three must be very proud."

Mandie turned and hugged her two Cherokee Indian friends together. Uncle Ned nodded and smiled.

Sallie squeezed Mandie's hand. "We are glad you are one of us," she said.

Mandie beamed. "I wonder if President McKinley

made a special point of sending us here, hoping we would find this," she commented.

"I don't know," Joe answered, "but I can tell it means a lot to you, so even if the President didn't plan it, I'm sure he would be happy to hear your reaction."

"Let's hurry and find Grandmother so we can tell her," Mandie said, starting down the stairs again. Paying little attention to the other inscribed stones, the young people and Uncle Ned made their way quickly down the remaining steps and hurried outside.

Mr. Adamson was pleased to see Mandie so excited about the Cherokee stone, and Mrs. Taft gave her granddaughter a knowing hug. After they all climbed back into the coach, Mandie and her companions told Mrs. Taft and Mr. Adamson about some of the rest of the stones they had seen, including the one from North Carolina.

Stopping for their noon meal at the Willard Hotel, they met several senators and cabinet officials whom Mr. Adamson knew, and Mandie swelled with pride each time she was introduced.

Then they stopped at the Smithsonian Institution, a red sandstone building that looked like a castle with nine towers.

Mr. Adamson helped Mandie and her grandmother out of the coach again. "Having seen your reaction to the stone donated by the Cherokees for the Washington Monument, I think there's something about this place you might be interested in," he said.

"What's that?" Mandie asked.

"Well, this institution is here today because of an eccentric British chemist named James Smithson," the President's assistant explained. "In 1829 he left as his legacy to the United States of America 105 bags containing over 100,000 gold sovereigns."

"Bags of gold?" Mandie asked in disbelief. "Like Joe and Sallie and I found in the cave?"

"Yes," Mr. Adamson replied with a grin. "And like you, Miss Amanda, he wanted the gold to be used for a noble purpose. He said it was to finance the founding of an institution to increase man's knowledge. So after the government took its time making up its mind how to do that, they built the Smithsonian Institution."

Mr. Adamson opened the door for them to enter the large building.

After spending a couple of hours looking at the inventions and scientific exhibits there, they entered the President's coach to return to the White House.

Mr. Adamson pulled the door closed behind him and sat opposite Mandie's grandmother. "Mrs. Taft, would you care to preside over tea in the President's parlor this afternoon?" he asked as the Negro driver urged the horses on. "Mrs. McKinley is not well enough to leave her room."

Mrs. Taft blinked her eyes several times. "Me? Preside over tea in the President's parlor?" she asked incredulously. "Why . . . yes . . . uh . . . I suppose I could."

Mr. Adamson smiled. "Thank you so much, ma'am," he said. "There will only be one more guest besides you people, and that will be Senator Morton. Perhaps you've heard of him. He's from Florida, and he's a close friend of the McKinleys. He should be arriving in town before teatime, and he will also be staying at the White House. In fact, the senator will be in the room on the other side of yours, Mrs. Taft."

Mandie leaned forward. "Will his wife be coming with him? Does he have any children?" she asked.

"No, Miss Amanda," Mr. Adamson replied. "His wife

died about three years ago, and they had no children. The senator is all alone now."

Mandie cast a quick glance at Joe. She couldn't help but want to play matchmaker. *I wonder what this man is like,* she thought.

Sallie touched Mandie's arm and gave her a cautious, knowing smile.

When they arrived at the White House, Uncle Ned and Mr. Adamson got out first to help the others down from the coach. Mr. Adamson closed the coach door. "There is a parlor near your rooms that you might want to use until teatime," he suggested. "In fact, feel free to use it whenever you wish while you're here. I'll ask Antoinette to show you where it is."

After the maid had taken them to the parlor, Mrs. Taft decided to rest until time to serve tea, and Uncle Ned went outside for some fresh air. Mandie hurried to her room to get Snowball; then the young people relaxed in the parlor.

Mandie cuddled her kitten to her and wandered around the room, examining the large urns, vases, and other furnishings. "This room sure is full of old things, isn't it?" she commented.

"Well, really, the whole White House is an antique," Joe reminded her. "Remember, it was finished enough for John Adams to move in, in 1800, and that's over a hundred years ago."

"Why don't we go look around the rest of the White House?" Mandie suggested.

"Do you think it would be all right?" Sallie asked.

"No," Joe said emphatically.

"I don't see why not," Mandie argued. She walked to the door. "Come on, Sallie. Go with me."

Sallie stood up uncertainly. "Where are you going?"

Joe got up and stood in front of the warm fire in the fireplace. "Mandie, you'd better stay here," he warned.

"I just want to walk down some of the hallways and look in the unoccupied rooms," she said to Sallie, ignoring Joe's remark. "After all, we've been all over Washington, D.C., but we haven't even had a tour of the place where we're staying yet," she argued.

As Sallie started toward the door, Mandie turned to Joe. "Are you coming?" she asked. "If you're not, I'll leave Snowball in here with you."

"Oh, no, you don't," Joe protested. He strode across the room to join the girls. "I suppose I'll go with you, but I'm warning you, you'd better not stir up any trouble."

Mandie led the way, and they roamed through the hallways of the White House, smiling at everyone they met and stopping to inspect the many pieces of furniture, vases, and bric-a-brac lining the walls. There was no sound coming from any of the rooms. No one seemed to be around except for the employees who occasionally passed them in the halls.

Then Joe found an elevator near the President's private quarters. "This is great!" he exclaimed. "It looks like one of those that works on water pressure. I've read about these things in a book my father gave me." But when he tried to operate the elevator, he couldn't get it to move. "Must be broken," he said, wiping his dusty hands on his pants.

The young people headed down the hallway. Mandie especially wanted to see the other rooms named for colors that her teacher had told her about. In a short time they found the Green Room and then the Blue Room with all their magnificent furnishings of matching colors.

Mandie's favorite was the Blue Room, where the walls were covered with blue silk the color of a robin's egg and patterned with leaves and little roses of a darker blue. The upholstery also had a rich-looking blue figured pattern. Above the windows, large panels of blue glass were decorated with gold scrollwork.

Mandie stared up at the ceiling, admiring the brass and nickel-plated crystal chandelier that hung from the center of the room. Dozens of electric light bulbs sparkled through the small hanging pieces of cut glass.

Joe said he liked the feel underfoot of the soft simple-patterned carpeting that extended from wall to wall.

As they continued down hallways, they found a room with heavy, ornately carved double doors. They stopped to look. Mandie heard something and set Snowball down, motioning for the others to listen. But suddenly the voices rose angrily.

"This has gone far enough," boomed a deep voice from within the closed room. "It is time to do something!"

"Yes, I say we approach the President about it," a higher pitched male voice agreed.

The three young people looked at each other in alarm.

"Humph! What good will it do to approach the President?" mumbled a gravelly voice. "I say we get on with it and kill them all!"

The young people gasped and reached for each other in fright. Who could be saying such things? Mandie touched her finger to her lips in warning, then quietly grasped the doorknob in front of them. With all her strength she tried to turn it, but it wouldn't budge.

The voices argued on.

"Kill them all!" the first voice shouted.

"Traitors, that's what they are!" cried the second.

"Worse than traitors," grumbled the third.

"Let's get on with it, then," the first voice urged. "We will meet right here at sundown. Now let's go home!"

The young people frantically scrambled for a hiding place. Mandie tried another door and pushed it open. Holding it for the other two to enter, she kept an eye on the hallway to see if anyone was coming.

Sallie surveyed the room lined with shelves and shelves of books. "This must be the library," she said. "Look at all these books!"

Mandie pulled the door closed, leaving it open just a crack. "Shhh!" she hushed the others. "Let's see who comes down the hallway!"

Joe and Sallie crept over to stand behind Mandie. They all watched but no one came. Then they heard heavy footsteps retreating in the opposite direction.

"Aw, shucks," Mandie said. "They've gone the other way. It's too late to see them." Pushing the door open, she looked in the direction of the double doors, but the hallway turned at that point.

The young people went back into the library and sat down in some comfortable chairs by a window.

Sallie looked worried. "What are we going to do?" she asked. "Those men are going to kill some people."

Mandie shook her head slowly. "If we tell anybody, they won't believe us," she said.

"Besides," Joe added, "it's none of our business. We shouldn't have been eavesdropping."

"You are right, Joe," Sallie agreed. "We did not have permission to wander off."

"But is that as important as the fact that those men are planning to kill somebody?" Mandie argued. "I wonder why they had the doors locked."

"To keep meddlers like us out," Joe said tartly.

"Evidently, they did not want anyone to hear what they were saying," Sallie agreed.

Suddenly Mandie looked around the room and jumped up. "Snowball!" she exclaimed. "Where is Snowball?"

Joe glanced around in exasperation. "I knew that cat would run off somewhere," he groaned.

Sallie rose and looked under the chairs. "We had better look for him," she said. "This house is so large, he could be lost for days."

"Come on," Mandie said, rushing to the door.

But as they ran out into the hallway, they almost bumped into Isabelle carrying Snowball.

"Your kitten was lost." The young maid said, handing Snowball to Mandie. "I came looking for you to go to tea."

"Thank you, Isabelle," Mandie replied with a sigh. "I just now missed him." She scowled at the kitten and gave her a good scolding.

Following the maid to the President's parlor, they found Mrs. Taft already there waiting. There was also a handsome older man with silvery gray hair sitting on the settee opposite her. He rose as they entered the room.

*Senator Morton*, Mandie thought. Then she whispered quickly under her breath, "Let's not tell anybody anything about those men."

Mrs. Taft introduced the gentleman to the young people, and Mandie instantly liked him. He would make a good match for her grandmother, she decided. And her grandmother needed a husband.

As Mrs. Taft poured the tea, Mandie's mind drifted back to the voices they had heard. At the earliest possible moment, they would have to go back to that room and see what was inside.

# *Chapter 11 / Mystery in the Night*

The activities of the rest of the day kept the young people busy, so they didn't have time to go back to the room where they had heard voices. That night there was a dinner with about fifty guests in the formal dining room.

President McKinley had seated the young people near him, and Mandie enjoyed talking with him. Mrs. McKinley still wasn't feeling well, he had told them, but he thought she would be able to attend the ceremonies the next day if she rested now.

Just before dinner was to be served, the President tapped on his glass for attention. "Ladies and gentlemen," he said, raising his bushy eyebrows, "as you know, the occasion of this dinner is to honor these three young people for their good work."

Mandie, Sallie, and Joe looked at each other in dismay. They had not known this would happen. Mandie felt embarrassed, and she sensed her friends felt the same. Mandie caught sight of Uncle Ned near the far end of the table. He smiled and clasped his hands for her to see as the President continued.

"Now I'm sure you'd all like to hear from the young

people themselves exactly what happened." President McKinley turned to Mandie. "Miss Amanda, would you please tell these people how you came to find the gold? And then maybe you can tell us what happened afterward."

Mandie could feel the color rushing to her cheeks as she looked up at the President. "But, President McKinley, sir," Mandie began softly, "we just found the gold in a cave in the Nantahala Mountains."

The President smiled. "Please, dear, won't you stand up so everyone can hear you?" he urged.

Mandie slowly rose on shaky legs and looked around the table. She looked over at her grandmother sitting beside Senator Morton. She smiled to herself. President McKinley must have had the same idea for matchmaking to seat them together like that.

As she nervously cleared her throat, she felt fifty pairs of eyes on her. And when she tried to speak, nothing came out.

Then Joe, who was sitting next to her, gave her a nudge. "Just tell them the same way we told our parents and friends," he whispered. "Hurry up."

Mandie cleared her throat again and braced her hands on the edge of the table. "Well, you see, it was like this," she began, speaking rapidly. "We got lost in a cave, and we found this pile of gold in there. When we finally got out, we went home and told everybody about it . . . and . . ." She faltered and glanced at Joe.

"Tsali," Joe whispered, trying to help her. "Tell them about him."

"Oh, yes, Tsali," Mandie said. "He was the Indian warrior who put the gold in the cave. He hid there for awhile and scratched a message on the cave wall, saying that the gold was for the Cherokee people after the white people left. He gave himself up when the white men promised not to harm anyone else."

Mandie took a deep breath. "But they didn't keep their promise," she continued. "They killed him and his whole family except for one small son. When we found the gold, we tried to give it to the Cherokees, but they refused to have anything to do with it. They just told me to do something with it. So, since I knew they needed a hospital, we decided to build a hospital with it. That's all." She collapsed in her chair, her cheeks burning with embarrassment.

Instantly, the room rang with applause, and after a moment, the President stood again. "Now, let's hear from the other young lady, who is, by the way, a full-blooded Cherokee. She is also the granddaughter of my old friend, Ned Sweetwater, sitting down there." He motioned to the old Indian. "He was the one who told me about the gold. Now, Miss Sallie Sweetwater, would you please tell us what you know about it?"

Mandie looked at Uncle Ned in surprise. *So he knows the President*, she thought. *I'm finding out a lot of things I didn't know before.*

Sallie trembled nervously as she stood and spoke, but she added little to what Mandie had already said. After another round of applause President McKinley introduced Joe for his version of the story.

To Mandie's surprise, Joe stood up straight and tall and looked the other guests in the face as he related his story. "It was like Mandie told you," he said. "We got lost in that cave, and it turned out to be the cave that the Indian warrior Tsali had hidden in. He had left the gold there and written a message on the wall, saying, 'This gold left here for good of Cherokee after white man makes peace. This gold belongs to us who are hiding here to save our lives. Curse on the white man who takes it.' Then he signed his name—Tsali."

Joe shoved his hands deep into his pockets. "After we got the gold out, Uncle Ned and Mandie's Great Uncle Wirt went back to the cave to try to chisel out the message and save it for history. But the whole cave fell in, and the message was lost. They were lucky to get out alive. My father, who is a doctor, is overseeing the construction of the hospital for Mandie while she is away at school. He says it should be finished by springtime. Thank you, Mr. President, ladies and gentlemen."

Joe sat down amid a roar of applause. Mandie was proud of him. She had never seen him in such a situation, and she decided he would make a good courtroom lawyer.

The dinner lasted several hours. When it was over and everyone except Senator Morton had left, Mrs. Taft ordered the young people to bed. They would need to get up early the next morning to attend church with the President. The First Lady would also go with them if she had sufficiently recovered.

"We older people are going to have coffee in the President's parlor, but you young ones must get to bed immediately. You want to be fresh for tomorrow," Mrs. Taft told them. "And, Amanda, you promised Miss Prudence you would study while you were away from school, so I suggest you take about thirty minutes for that and then get into bed."

"Yes, Grandmother. I will," Mandie assured her. Then turning to the senator, she said, "Good night, Senator Morton. I hope you sleep well."

After telling all the young people good night, the senator offered his arm to Mrs. Taft, and the adults headed for the President's parlor.

Isabelle appeared in the corridor, and offered to help Mandie and her friends find their rooms again. As the young people followed her, Mandie asked, "Isabelle, do you think you could get something to eat for Snowball?" she asked. "He hasn't had any dinner, and I'd guess he's meowing like crazy after being shut up in my room all this time."

"Do not worry, Miss Amanda," Isabelle replied, continuing down the hallway. "Mr. Snowball has had a big supper. I saw to it myself. He's probably fast asleep by now."

When they reached their rooms, Mandie peeked into the one she was sharing with Sallie. There, curled up in the middle of the big bed was Snowball, sound asleep. Isabelle said good night and continued down the hall.

Mandie paused in the doorway, then turned to her friends. "Don't you think we ought to go look in that room where those men were talking today?" she asked.

"No," Joe said firmly. "Your grandmother told us to go to bed, and that's where you'd better go right now. Good night." He strode down the hallway a short distance to the room he was occupying.

Mandie turned to Sallie and shrugged. Then the two girls went into their room, closed the door, and began getting ready for bed.

"Maybe we can go look tomorrow sometime," Mandie suggested.

"Maybe," Sallie agreed. "But we do not want to do anything we should not."

Mandie felt a little frustrated, but she knew Joe and

Sallie were right. "Of course, Sallie," she said. Then taking her history book from her school bag, she sat down in one of the big comfortable chairs. "I have to do a little studying, so you go ahead to bed."

After saying good night, Sallie crawled under the covers and was soon sound asleep. Mandie read for awhile, but her eyes kept closing, so she finally gave up. Putting her history book back in the bag, she stood up and stretched, then carefully slid into bed to avoid waking her friend. Snowball curled up at her feet.

It seemed as if she had been asleep only a short time when a noise awakened her. She raised up on one elbow to listen. The noise seemed to be coming from the yard outside the window. Being careful not to wake Sallie, Mandie slipped out of bed, tiptoed over to the window, and looked out into the darkness. Snowball followed her.

A few gaslight lampposts by the driveway cast a faint light across the yard. As Snowball rubbed around her ankles, Mandie squinted into the darkness but couldn't see a thing. She was about to go back to bed when a strange figure appeared on the lawn.

Mandie gasped. It was George Washington again! And he was walking across the yard. Snatching a shawl from a nearby chair, she hurried out the door, banging it against the wall, and raced downstairs to get outside. Snowball ran after her. She knew the door had made a loud noise, but she hoped it hadn't awakened anyone.

By the time she made her way down the long hallways and reached a side door, she was panting, out of breath. Pushing the door open, she ran across the lawn toward where she had seen the strange figure. She ran and ran and looked all around but couldn't see a single soul. George Washington had just plain disappeared.

Hearing someone call her name, she gasped and turned to see her old friend, Uncle Ned, peeking out from behind a tree in the darkness. He started toward her. "Papoose, cold out here," he called to her. "Go back inside."

Suddenly she realized just how cold she was with only her nightgown and the thin shawl she had grabbed at the last minute. She shivered. "Uncle Ned!" she cried, starting toward him.

Then she saw her grandmother hurrying across the lawn toward them with a lantern. "Amanda, what are you doing out here at this time of night?" she called.

Mandie knew she was in trouble now. Her grandmother would demand to know what she was doing. *Oh, well*, she thought, *I might as well tell her*. But she spoke to Uncle Ned first. "Did you see anyone come across the yard ahead of me just now, Uncle Ned?" she asked as Mrs. Taft caught up with them.

"No, Papoose. No one here," Uncle Ned replied. "I out for breath of air. No one come."

"Amanda," Mrs. Taft demanded, "what are you doing out here? You're going to catch your death of cold. Get back inside immediately."

"Grandmother, I thought I saw George Washington walking across the yard," Mandie explained, realizing how foolish it must sound.

"Oh, dear child, are you running a fever, or are you sleepwalking?" Mrs. Taft asked anxiously. "George Washington has been dead and buried many a year now, dear."

"I don't think I was imagining things, Grandmother," Mandie replied.

Mrs. Taft held the lantern high and grabbed Mandie's hand. "You must have been having a dream," she said. "Let's all get back inside at once. It's too cold out here to be wandering around this time of night."

Mandie picked up Snowball and held him close.

"Yes, time me go in, too," Uncle Ned said, leading them back inside the White House.

After saying good night to Uncle Ned in the hallway outside their rooms, Mandie asked her grandmother what brought her outside.

"Why, you must have banged that door loud enough to wake the dead when you went out," Mrs. Taft explained. "I got up to see what was going on, and there was Sallie, sound asleep—bless her heart. I'll never know how she slept through that loud bang. But you were missing. Then I just happened to see you through the window." She stroked Mandie's hair. "Now get in bed, dear, and don't you get out again tonight, do you hear?"

"Yes, ma'am," Mandie said reluctantly. "Good night." Going to her room, she closed the door and set Snowball down, then slipped into the warm bed.

But she couldn't get to sleep right away. For a long time she lay awake thinking. She didn't believe she was just having nightmares or imagining things, but what else could it be? No one else had seen anyone who even looked like George Washington. Besides, it was true—George Washington had died a long time ago. How could he be walking around the White House?

She sighed deeply. Since no one believed her, she decided she wouldn't mention it to anyone again. She would just keep it to herself and stay on the lookout for him.

---

When Mandie awoke the next morning, the first thing that came to her mind was the incident of the night before. She lay there for a moment, wondering if the whole thing had really happened. Suddenly she was determined to find out.

Noticing that someone had already built a roaring fire in the huge fireplace, she jumped out of bed, grabbed her robe, and sat down in front of it. Sallie stirred and sat up.

Mandie turned to look at her friend. "It must be too early to get up, Sallie," she said. "I'm sorry if I woke you."

Sallie threw back the heavy covers and swung around to sit on the side of the big bed. Finding her robe, she joined Mandie in front of the fire. "It is never too early for me," the Indian girl said as the firelight splashed on their faces. "I like to get up early. It's so nice and quiet and clean early in the morning."

"I like to get up early, too," Mandie replied, "but I thought maybe after our big day yesterday, you might want to sleep later." Mandie kept debating whether to tell her friend about the figure she had seen the night before on the lawn. Finally she decided against it, at least for now. "Let's get dressed and see if we can find the dining room," she continued. "For some reason I'm starving."

"I am, too," Sallie said. "I imagine my grandfather is already in the dining room."

"Joe, too, probably," Mandie agreed.

When the girls finally found their way to the dining room, both Joe and Uncle Ned were there, digging into enormous breakfasts.

Joe glanced up. "Good morning, sleepyheads," he greeted them.

"Good morning," Mandie replied. "We're not exactly sleepyheads. No one called us for breakfast." The girls pulled out two chairs across from Joe and Uncle Ned and sat down. "Besides, we kept late hours last night."

Uncle Ned smiled at Mandie. "Did Papoose find what she look for last night?" he asked.

"No, Uncle Ned," Mandie answered quickly. Not wanting Joe to know anything about the incident the night before, she quickly changed the subject. "We are supposed to go to church with the President today," she said brightly. "I hope Mrs. McKinley is well enough to go."

"I do, too," Sallie agreed. "She has been ill so much, I hear."

Joe seemed to understand what Mandie was trying to do. "What was Papoose looking for last night?" he teased.

"Nothing, really," Mandie answered. "Are we going back to look at that room today?" She didn't want to say too much about this matter, either, with Uncle Ned there.

"I don't think we'll have time," Joe said. "The inauguration is tomorrow, and it seems today is crammed full of things to do."

"Many people coming to stay in White House," Uncle Ned told them. "President invite whole houseful. Come today."

"And I suppose we won't have much of a chance to get away if the halls are going to be running over with people," Mandie moaned.

Just then a maid in a starched white uniform came over to where the girls were sitting. "What would you two young ladies like for breakfast?" she asked.

Mandie looked up at her. "Scrambled eggs and grits—do you have grits?" she asked.

The maid smiled. "We certainly do. The President ordered them just for you people."

"Thanks," Mandie said with a grin. "I'll have scrambled eggs and grits and a piece of bacon or ham, whatever you have. And coffee to drink."

Sallie ordered the same, and the maid went back to the kitchen.

Mandie stared after her. "The President certainly is a thoughtful man," she said.

"Yes, he thought up all kinds of things for us to do between now and when we leave on Tuesday," Joe remarked.

"Like what?" Mandie asked.

"Like going to church," Joe counted on his long, bony fingers as he named the activities, "coming back to eat, an excursion to a museum, back again for afternoon tea, a concert in the East Room, supper in the formal dining room with all those other house guests, and—"

"How do you know all this?" Mandie asked.

"Uncle Ned told me," Joe answered.

The maid brought Mandie and Sallie's breakfast and placed it before them. After a short prayer of thanks, Mandie looked at her grits curiously. She laughed. "They certainly don't know how to cook grits," she said. "This looks like soup."

"There're lots of things these people don't know that we know—like the conversation we overheard," Joe teased, "and dead people you've seen walking the halls of the White House."

"Joe Woodard," Mandie protested. "I'll have you know I saw George Washington again last night walking across the lawn. I didn't just imagine it. I saw him with my own two eyes."

Sallie and Joe looked at each other in surprise.

"You did?" Joe questioned.

"Are you sure, Mandie?" Sallie asked.

Mandie wished she hadn't given herself away. She had

not meant to tell Joe and Sallie about the figure she had seen—at least not yet, anyway.

Uncle Ned spoke up. "Papoose see," he said. "I on lawn, too, last night."

Mandie noticed that he didn't say he saw George Washington, but he was trying to imply that he did. She smiled up at him.

Joe leaned forward toward Mandie. "Well, what are you going to do about it?" he asked.

Mandie looked straight into Joe's brown eyes. "Nothing," she said. "At least not right now."

"I know. There's always later," Joe replied, turning back to his breakfast.

Later that morning as they all left for church, Senator Morton escorted Mrs. Taft, and Mandie quietly smiled to herself. Things were going well between them, she thought. The First Lady felt a little better, so she attended church with all of them, too.

The President was Methodist, Mandie learned, and she admired his kindness and the way he lived. *The President of the United States should set an example for the rest of the country*, she thought.

During the service at the church, the minister mentioned the forthcoming inauguration and the capable way the President had handled his first term. After the sermon, the congregation stood in respect as the President left the church building.

When they returned for the noon meal, the White House overflowed with guests as predicted. People were rushing every which way.

The dining room was crammed full for the meal, and the young people hurried to finish, hoping they could sneak around to the room where they had heard the angry voices. But there was no way. The President rose from the table and announced that carriages would be at the front door for sightseeing.

Mandie went over to her grandmother. "Do we have to go on the sightseeing trip, Grandmother?" she asked. "Can't we just stay here and relax?"

"I'm sorry, dear, but you'll have to go," Mrs. Taft replied. "When you are in another person's home, you must do whatever has been planned, especially when it is the President of the United States that you are visiting. Amanda, you have to understand what an honor this is for you to even be here. Now run along, all of you, and get your wraps quickly," she said, turning back to Senator Morton, who was at her elbow.

Mandie made a face as she joined her friends. "You both heard?" she asked. "We have to go."

"Yes," Sallie nodded.

"That's all right," Joe brightened. "Maybe we can skip teatime later."

Mandie smiled. "We'll see," she said doubtfully.

But her grandmother required her to attend everything, and before Mandie knew it, the day was over. And they hadn't had any time to investigate.

*Maybe tomorrow?* she thought as she drifted off to sleep.

# Chapter 12 / The Big Day

Inauguration Day began with a dark sky, and as Mandie got dressed in her finest blue gown, she listened to the bands outside warming up and entertaining the crowds that had already started to gather along President McKinley's route to the Capitol. But Mandie worried about the ceremonies on the east portico of the Capitol building.

At breakfast the young people discussed the situation. What would happen if it poured down rain—especially since the President had so recently been sick?

Mandie served herself some coffee from the pot the maid had left on the table. "I think the President would have to change his plans at the last minute and hold the ceremonies inside somewhere," she said.

Joe dug into a plate heaped with bacon and eggs and pancakes. "Maybe he'll come in for breakfast while we're here and we can ask him," he replied.

"I do not believe the President would stand outside in the pouring rain to be sworn in again as President," Sallie mused. "This is his second term, and I imagine he had lots of celebrations the first time he was inaugurated."

"You know these politicians like to make a big to-do about everything," Joe said. "And I imagine President McKinley is as big a politician as any of them when it comes to putting on a big splash."

"I just wish he didn't have everything planned minute to minute where we can't have any time alone," Mandie said between bites of hot biscuit. "Those men in that room, whoever they were, could have already gone out and done something terrible. Remember they said they were going to 'get on with it,' and they were talking about killing people."

Sallie held her cup with both hands and stared into the steamy, dark coffee. "Yes, they might have even done it already," she said.

"And we don't know who they were talking about, so there's nothing we can do about it," Joe added.

But even as they prepared to leave for the inauguration, Mandie still hoped they could investigate later on that day.

About ten-thirty that morning, when the President left the White House, he took off his silk top hat and waved it at the cheering crowd in the street. Then he climbed into his coach for a quick ride to the Capitol. The streets along the route to the Capitol seemed alive with elaborate decorations of red, white, and blue.

The inaugural ceremony greatly impressed Mandie and her friends. The President had invited them and many of his other house guests to sit with him during the proceedings on the east portico. The sky remained overcast, but there was no rain at noon when President McKinley stood to be sworn into office for the second time. Raising his right hand, he placed his left on a large Bible. Mrs. McKinley sat behind the President, smiling proudly, as Chief Justice Melville Weston Fuller administered the presidential oath. The young people listened carefully.

"I, William McKinley, do solemnly swear," the President repeated in all seriousness, "that I will faithfully execute the Office of President of the United States, and will, to the best of my ability, preserve, protect, and defend the Constitution of the United States."

The crowd cheered. Then as a light rain began to fall, the President addressed the spectators huddled under heavy black umbrellas. "My fellow citizens . . ." the President began, telling them what an honor it was to be elected a second time.

After the speech came the inaugural parade, which the young people watched from the street among thousands of other rain-drenched spectators. Mandie and her friends enjoyed the big brass bands and ranks of men in military uniform.

As the rain grew heavier, many people either ran for shelter or left altogether. The parade picked up speed, and the young people hurried behind the marching bands, making their way back to the White House.

The President and Mrs. McKinley, as well as most of the other White House guests, including Mrs. Taft and Senator Morton, had already returned by the time Mandie and her friends arrived. Coming into the entrance hall, they quickly removed their wet coats and hats, smoothed back their hair, and hurried to their rooms to change.

Mandie stood in front of the mirror, drying her hair with a towel. "Look how wet my hair is," she moaned. "My hat didn't do much good."

"My hair is very wet also," Sallie replied. Quickly wrapping it in a towel, she changed dresses.

"It was worth it, though," Mandie commented. "I feel as if I'm in fairyland or something—that things just aren't real. We've done and seen so much! I can't wait to get back to school and tell Celia all about it."

"And I will tell my grandmother about everything," Sallie said, buttoning another of the fancy dresses Mandie's mother had bought for her.

Mandie stood back and admired her Indian friend. The pale yellow dress looked pretty against her bronze skin and black hair. "You know we still haven't had a chance to put on our old dresses," she said. "We just keep going and going and putting on more and more fancy clothes. It's really funny," She burst into laughter and fell onto the bed.

Sallie looked at her curiously. "Mandie, what is so funny?" she asked.

But Mandie couldn't quit laughing. The more she laughed, the funnier it became. Soon Sallie began giggling at Mandie, which made Mandie laugh all the more.

Finally, Sallie regained control and looked at her friend with concern. "Mandie, are you all right?" she asked.

"Sure I am," Mandie replied through tears of laughter. "It's just that I'm so wound up, I had to have a good laugh."

"That is fine, but I think we had better hurry," Sallie warned. "Here, let's go over by the fireplace, and I'll help you dry your hair."

As the two girls stood in the warmth of the fire, Sallie reached for the towel and began briskly rubbing her friend's long locks.

"Thanks, Sallie," Mandie said as the Indian girl finished. "I think it's dry now. I can brush it back. Let me find a dress to put on."

Taking down a new green silk dress from the wardrobe, Mandie hurriedly put it on, and Sallie buttoned up the back.

"I wonder where Joe is," Mandie said. She quickly combed through her damp hair and tied it back with a wide piece of green satin ribbon.

At that moment there was a knock on the door. "Are y'all ready yet?" Joe called from the hallway.

Mandie opened the door. "We're ready," she said. "What took you so long?"

The three young people headed toward the East Room where everyone was supposed to be.

Joe looked at her out of the corner of his eye. "I ran to look in that room where the men were talking, and—"

"You did?" Mandie interrupted. "How could you go without us?"

"Since I'm not a girl, it doesn't take me long to change clothes," Joe teased. "But anyway, the door was still locked, and I didn't even see anyone in the hallway down there."

When the young people entered the East Room, they found it full of people. Mrs. Taft and Senator Morton stood near the doorway, and Mrs. Taft saw them at once. "Dears, are you all right?" she asked. "I was beginning to wonder where you'd gone. We have just been told that the fireworks for the evening have been postponed because of the rain. Instead, a dramatic group will put on a skit. This was scheduled for the ball tonight, but since there is some free time now, the group will perform before we get dressed for the ball."

"Grandmother, are you sure you want me to go to the Inaugural Ball?" Mandie protested. "I've never been to a ball before."

"I know, dear," Mrs. Taft replied, "and I am giving you permission to stay just for the first part of it when the President and the First Lady lead things off." She turned to Joe and Sallie. "Of course you two will stay with Amanda all evening, won't you?"

Joe and Sallie nodded.

"Will my grandfather be there?" Sallie asked, looking around the room.

"Yes, dear, he will," Mrs. Taft assured her. "He's around here somewhere right now."

Just then Mandie heard music, and she raised her head. In the corner of the room a small orchestra had begun playing. The loud talking across the room quieted as the stringed instruments filled the room with gentle but happy music. Then the President stepped onto a small platform, and the conductor stopped the music.

The President looked around the room. "Ladies and gentlemen," he began, "please be seated. The play is about to begin. Thank you."

The adults took their time being seated, and the young people scrambled to find chairs near the front. Mandie spied her old Indian friend near the orchestra. "There's Uncle Ned," she told the others. "Let's go find a seat by him."

Hurrying across the room, they managed to find enough chairs by him just before a chord sounded from the orchestra and the curtain on the improvised stage slowly opened.

The young people watched as the actors, dressed in costumes from the Revolutionary War period began talking and moving about the stage.

Mandie listened intently to the dialogue, then caught her breath as a new character came on stage. It was

George Washington! The same George Washington figure she had seen in the hallway and on the lawn!

She nudged Joe and leaned forward. "Look!" she whispered. "There he is. I told you I wasn't imagining things! There's the George Washington I saw."

Joe stared at the characters on stage. "Of all things!" he said.

"That man certainly does look like the pictures I have seen of George Washington," Sallie agreed.

Uncle Ned nodded and turned back to watch the play.

Mandie smiled in self-satisfaction, then watched as the first scene ended and the curtain closed. Seconds later, it reopened, showing a group of men gathered around a table.

"This has gone far enough," said a short, stocky man with a vaguely familiar deep bass voice. "It is time to do something."

"Yes," replied a tall, slender man with a higher pitched voice. "I say we approach the President about it."

Mandie, Joe, and Sallie grabbed one another's hands in excitement. These were the men they had overheard in that locked room upstairs.

"Humph!" said a heavy man with a gravelly voice. "What good will it do to approach the President? I say we get on with it and kill them all!"

At last Mandie understood the dialogue. The men were talking about colonists who had turned Tories, or traitors, during the American Revolution. She sighed with relief, then settled back to enjoy the rest of the performance.

As soon as the skit was over, people began milling around again, visiting, but Mandie and her friends stayed near the stage.

"Just think," Mandie laughed, "we really thought those men in that room upstairs were going out to kill somebody."

"And you thought you had really seen George Washington," Joe teased. "But then I suppose you really did see him—at least the one in the play."

"The actor did look like the pictures of George Washington," Sallie added.

A few minutes later Mrs. Taft found the young people and informed them that they had one hour to get dressed for dinner and the ball immediately afterward.

"Then we'd better hurry," Mandie said. "It'll take awhile to put on all that finery I'm supposed to wear."

"Yes, at least one hour," Sallie agreed.

"My finery won't take me that long," Joe mocked in a high voice; "but I'll wait in my room for you girls," he told them.

Mrs. Taft started to leave, then called back to them. "Please be ready on time," she said. "I'm sure Isabelle will come and help you dress."

However, by the time Isabelle did knock on their door, the girls had already helped each other and were nearly ready.

"So sorry," Isabelle apologized. "It took me longer to help Mrs. Taft than I thought it would, but oh, you look so fine—like exquisite dolls. You do not need my help. I will go now," she said, closing the door behind her.

Mandie blushed slightly, but she had to admit she did feel pretty in her floor-length baby blue silk ball gown with little pink rosebuds cascading down the front. The neckline was lower than anything she had ever worn before, but since there was a matching silk shawl, she looped it high. Her dressy slippers matched her gown, and Sallie had threaded a matching blue ribbon through Mandie's blonde hair.

Sallie's floor-length gown was baby pink silk with lots of frills and lace on it. It had a higher neckline and long sleeves. She wore matching pink slippers and pulled her long, straight black hair back with a matching piece of lace.

The girls twirled admiringly in front of the full-length mirror.

"I feel so grown up tonight," Mandie said, flipping her skirt around. "I don't feel like twelve years old anymore. I feel sixteen tonight."

"I feel older, also." Sallie smiled at her reflection. "I wonder what my grandfather will say when he sees me."

Mandie laughed. "*I* wonder what he will look like in his new clothes," she remarked.

"Everyone will look pretty tonight," Sallie said. She paused for a moment, thinking. "Mandie, how many people will there be at this ball?" she asked.

"As far as I know, it's a private ball just for the house guests and a few other close friends of the President and First Lady," Mandie replied. "And we're all a part of this group of important people. Aren't we lucky?"

"Not really," Sallie said, straightening her long skirt for the dozenth time. "I will not be comfortable until I can remove these fine clothes."

A moment later Joe and Uncle Ned knocked on their door. When Mandie opened it, she noticed Senator Morton knocking on her grandmother's door. The girls stepped out into the hallway, carefully closing the door behind them to keep Snowball in, then watched in surprise as Mrs. Taft almost floated out of her room to take Senator Morton's arm.

Mrs. Taft looked like a queen in all her rich splendor. She wore a floor-length dark green satin dress and adorned herself with expensive gold, diamond, and emerald jewelry.

Senator Morton's eyes lit up when he saw her. Compliments flowed freely between all of them as they stood in the hallway for a few minutes.

Mandie looked up admiringly at Uncle Ned in his dark suit. She grabbed his old wrinkled hand. "You look wonderful, Uncle Ned. I didn't realize you were so handsome," she teased.

Uncle Ned didn't seem to know whether she was teasing or not.

"My grandfather, you *are* handsome," Sallie said proudly.

Joe stepped over to Mandie's side. "And you, young ladies, must have just stepped out of the fashion pages," he said.

"You, too, Joe," Mandie replied. "You don't look like the Joe Woodard I used to know."

Uncle Ned started down the hall. "Must go," he reminded them.

When they reached the dining room, Mandie felt self-conscious among all the rich, expensively dressed guests. Having grown up in a small cabin in the mountains, even her etiquette lessons at the Heathwoods' school didn't prepare her for associating with so many high-society people.

Then President McKinley came over to them, dressed in formal attire. "My, but you all look nice," he said. "I'm proud of you all in more ways than one."

"Thank you, Mr. McKinley," Mandie replied, and the others did the same. Then as the President moved on to speak to others nearby, Mandie felt embarrassed. "I don't think I should have called him Mr. McKinley," she realized. "I've only heard him addressed as Mr. President."

"That's all right. He knows we're just country crackers," Joe quipped.

They all laughed, then moved on to find their places at the dinner table.

Dinner conversation was lively, and Mandie thought she had never tasted such rich, delicious food and desserts as those set before her. She couldn't help but think that her schoolmates back in Asheville would be jealous if they could see how royally she was being treated. Mandie definitely was feeling special.

After dinner, everyone moved back into the East Room where the orchestra was again playing soft, wonderful music. Mandie swayed with the tempo and enjoyed the swish of her long dress around her feet. She looked up when the President again took the platform. He addressed his guests briefly, telling them how glad he was to have his special friends with him on this important night. Then after the First Lady said a few words, the ball was underway.

Mandie still felt that Mrs. McKinley looked pale, but the First Lady seemed to be caught up in the excitement and had a bit more color in her cheeks than she had had the day before.

As the guests twirled around them, Mandie and her friends had a great time drinking pink punch from crystal glasses and standing around, catching snatches of other people's conversations. Sauntering over to a roped-off corner where Mrs. Taft sat talking with Senator Morton, Mandie overheard her grandmother inviting the senator to visit her in Asheville.

"Thank you, Mrs. Taft," the senator replied. "I don't know exactly when, but maybe when we take our next break here in Washington, I could stop by on my way home to Florida."

"Oh, Senator, that would be wonderful. I look forward to showing you our town," Mrs. Taft replied. Looking around, she noticed the young people standing nearby and blushed slightly. "Amanda, dear, I believe it is time for you and your friends to go to your rooms," she said. "It is getting late."

The young people looked at each other knowingly.

"Good night," Mandie said. She turned to leave, then stopped and turned back. "When do we leave tomorrow, Grandmother?" she asked.

"Immediately after breakfast, dear," Mrs. Taft replied. "Remember, we're stopping to spend the night with Celia's mother again. Good night now. Good night, Sallie and Joe. I'll see y'all in the morning."

Mandie led the way as the young people headed out of the East Room. Once in the hallway, she started dancing around happily. "We're going home tomorrow!" she said in a sing-song voice. "We're going home."

Joe looked at her curiously. "I thought you wanted to come here."

"I did, but now I'm ready to go back to school. I can't wait to tell all those girls about the President and everything we've seen in Washington, D.C. They are going to be so jealous!"

Joe and Sallie frowned at each other.

"Besides," Mandie continued, "Celia and I still have another mystery to solve back at school."

Sallie shrugged her shoulders. "I think I have had

enough mysteries," she said. "My grandfather and I will leave tomorrow morning also. And I will be glad to get home and into some comfortable clothes."

"Amen!" Joe echoed.

## Chapter 13 / What Happened at the Farm?

After saying goodbye to the President and First Lady the next morning, Mandie rode with her grandmother in the President's coach to the train station. Because of their stopover to spend the night with Celia's mother and another long train ride from Richmond to Asheville, it was late the next day when Ben met them at the depot and took Mandie back to the Heathwoods' school.

Mandie opened the front door and entered, with Ben right behind her. Ben set her luggage inside the vestibule, told her goodbye, and left to take Mrs. Taft home.

Mandie looked around, disappointed that no one was waiting for her. Hurrying down the hallway, she found the headmistress in her office. "I'm back, Miss Prudence," she announced excitedly. "I had such a wonderful time! The President is so nice, and the First Lady is absolutely beautiful, and—"

"That's enough for tonight, Amanda," Miss Prudence interrupted. She stood and walked around to the front of her desk. "Get up to your room now and study until curfew. I'll ask Uncle Cal to bring up your bags. Good night."

She walked out of her office and headed down the hallway.

Mandie's enthusiasm was deflated. Reluctantly, she turned toward the stairway. Then she remembered Celia. Celia would be eager to hear her exciting experiences. Mandie took the steps two at a time.

Pushing open the door to their room, Mandie found Celia sprawled with a book on the rug in front of the crackling fire.

Celia jumped up. "Mandie!" she squealed in delight, hugging her friend. "Tell, tell, tell! What happened? Did you have a good time?"

Mandie shed her coat and hat, then sat down in front of the fire with Celia. "Oh, I had a wonderful time," she said, her blue eyes dancing, "but I can tell you right now, I'm just plain tuckered out. I have never been so busy in my life. There was something going on every minute of every day until late at night. And guess what? The President had invited Joe and Sallie and Uncle Ned, too!"

"Please tell me about every minute of it, please," Celia begged.

Mandie talked about her trip, and the sightseeing, and all the mysteries along the way until they heard the curfew bell. Then suddenly Mandie realized that Uncle Cal hadn't brought up her bags yet. "I guess I'm going to have to go down and get my luggage myself," she said, a little irritated.

But just then there was a knock on the door. "Oh, maybe not." Mandie laughed. Opening the door, she found Uncle Cal standing there with her bags.

He grinned. "Sorry it took me so long, Missy," he apologized, "but Miz Prudence, she say she give you a extra hour after de bell ring to git unpacked." He placed the baggage in the corner.

"Oh, thank you, Uncle Cal," Mandie said excitedly. "I've just got to tell you about my visit with the President and—"

Uncle Cal held up his hand. "Sorry again, Missy," he replied, "but Miz Prudence, she done give me strict orders to git up here and right back. She need me downstairs right away." He headed for the door. "I hears 'bout dat President man tomorrow, Missy. Good night."

Mandie sighed. "Good night, Uncle Cal," she said. "I'll see you and Aunt Phoebe tomorrow."

As the old Negro man closed the door behind him, Mandie turned to Celia. "That reminds me. Have things been normal since I've been gone? Has Aunt Phoebe been gone anymore, or Miss Hope?"

"Everything is back to normal," Celia assured her. "I haven't missed anyone, anyway. So if they have been gone, I didn't know it. I haven't seen the mouse again, either, and April Snow has behaved, too, would you believe it?"

"I hope it stays that way, just normal like it should be," Mandie replied as she began unpacking.

Celia helped her hang up clothes and put things away in drawers as they continued talking.

"I'd still like to know what was going on with everyone disappearing for days at a time," Mandie said. "We know it has something to do with the farm, but what? If only we could find out what Miss Hope said to Miss Prudence at the dining room table that first night she disappeared . . ."

When the girls finally finished the unpacking, they got ready for bed, blew out the light, and slid under the covers to talk late into the night.

At breakfast the next morning, to Mandie's surprise,

Miss Prudence welcomed Mandie back and announced that Mandie would tell everyone about her journey after supper that night. All the students were required to meet in the parlor.

Mandie smiled a self-important smile and only barely noticed her fellow students' looks that said, Who does she think she is?

As the day floated by, Mandie had quite a bit of catching up to do in her class work, so she had no time to talk to anyone. When it was finally time to go to the parlor after supper, she and Celia were the last ones to arrive. They stopped in surprise in the parlor doorway.

Besides the girls from her own school, the room was crammed with students from Mr. Chadwick's boys' school, who had come to hear about her visit with the President. *How could Miss Prudence do this to her?*

Mandie struggled for a moment, embarrassed yet flattered that Miss Prudence thought her journey important enough to invite all these people to hear her. She smiled weakly at the headmistress and Miss Hope, who sat at a table off to the side of the room.

Mandie was certain Tommy Patton was in the group. They had become friends on other visits between the two schools. But she was afraid to look for him. In fact, she avoided the eyes of all the listeners as she nervously took a place in the corner of the crowded room and began relating her adventure.

"First of all," she said, her voice quavering, "I want to thank Miss Prudence and Miss Hope for allowing me to take leave from school." She stopped and cleared her throat. "President McKinley is a wonderful man. And his wife is so warm and friendly. As you probably know, my grandmother went with me. And the President also invited my friends, Joe Woodard and Sallie Sweetwater and Uncle Ned, my old Cherokee friend."

There was a snicker in the group, and Mandie caught sight of April Snow in the back row making a face .

Miss Prudence rapped on the table and stood up. "We will have none of that now," she said sternly. "You will maintain silence until Amanda has finished. In fact, I would suggest that you pay close attention because I might just give a test on her speech."

The students looked at each other and frowned.

*Oh, no,* Mandie said to herself. *The girls will hate me.*

Miss Prudence remained standing, keeping a watchful eye on the students. "Please continue, Amanda," she said.

Mandie tried to make it short. But she had to tell them about the beautiful rooms in the White House, climbing the 898 steps of the Washington Monument, and seeing all the exhibits in the Smithsonian Institution. And Miss Prudence, Miss Hope, and Mr. Chadwick kept asking questions now and then, making her go into more detail about everything she had seen and learned. The students remained quiet, but Mandie wasn't sure they were really interested.

Finally, when she could think of nothing else to say, she turned to the headmistress. "Thank you, Miss Prudence," she said, sinking down into the chair behind her.

"Thank *you*, Amanda," Miss Prudence replied. "You have given an interesting account of your visit." She turned to address all the students. "Young ladies and gentlemen, we will serve tea in the dining room now, but since there are so many of us, you may bring your refreshments back here or take them into the hallway while you visit with one another. Please follow me."

As the students moved through the line, they all seemed to avoid Mandie. They looked at her out of the corners of their eyes and stayed out of her path.

But Tommy Patton and his friend Robert Rogers singled out Mandie and Celia to discuss the Washington trip and the latest happenings at the two schools. With the cold shoulder Mandie was getting from the other girls, she was glad to talk to Tommy as they waited in line. Tommy was a tall, handsome, boy with dark brown eyes, and Mandie always enjoyed being with him.

Tommy smiled down at her. "I've never been to Washington, D.C.," he said. "You certainly did make the inauguration and everything sound interesting."

"Thank you, Tommy," Mandie replied, accepting a cup of tea and a small cake from Aunt Phoebe. The others did likewise and the four of them wandered out into the less-crowded hallway to talk.

"I don't think it's very interesting to the other girls, though," Mandie said sadly. "Miss Prudence has seen to that with the threat of a test."

Robert smiled shyly at Celia and took a drink of his tea. "I don't think she really meant it," he said.

"I certainly hope not," Mandie replied.

Tommy leaned over to Mandie and spoke softly so that no one outside their group could hear him. "Pardon me for saying so, but Miss Prudence ought to know that a test would make the other girls despise you," he said. "They're bound to be jealous enough already that the President invited you to the White House."

Mandie laughed nervously. "Well, let them be jealous," she returned. "I was the one the President invited. After all, most of these girls have lots of money, but what have they ever done for other people? They haven't built a hospital for the Indians or anything."

The boys and Celia eyed Mandie with concern. What was happening to her?

---

In the days that followed, the other students avoided Mandie more and more because Miss Prudence *did* give a test on Mandie's account of her trip to Washington. Mandie tried to pretend she didn't notice their reactions, but no one would even talk to her. Even Celia seemed a little distant, not her usual warm, bubbly self.

April Snow snickered every time she saw Mandie in the hallway—as long as the schoolmistresses weren't in sight. Sometimes she would mock Mandie, saying things like, "Princess Amanda! She went to visit the President!"

Mandie was furious, but she didn't answer April. She simply tried to avoid her.

One afternoon between classes Mandie overheard two other students talking.

"I wish she had never even come to this school," Etrulia Batson said with disgust. "She thinks she's so important."

The other girl said, "I wish I could have been there in Washington just to see that little mountain girl make a fool out of herself, for all she knows about society functions," she replied.

Mandie turned and quietly slipped into an empty classroom. Tears welled in her eyes as she thought about what they had said. *Why does everybody hate me so?* she wondered. *It isn't my fault that Miss Prudence decided to give that test.* She wiped her eyes and took a deep breath. *I'm not going to let it bother me,* she told herself. *The President thinks I'm special. What difference does it make what these girls think? They're just jealous.*

After all the catching up she had to do on her schoolwork and the way the girls were treating her, Mandie was really looking forward to Easter holidays. But a few days before they were to begin, Miss Prudence announced that the school would not close for the usual week. The girls had already missed too much school-time because of the flu epidemic during the winter, she said. They would stay at school and have Good Friday and Easter Monday observances there.

Disappointed with Miss Prudence's decision, Mandie found some comfort in the fact that she and Celia were at least allowed to attend church and spend the day with her grandmother on Easter Sunday. Easter came on April seventh that year, and the weather was already warm. Leaves sprouted on the trees, and flowers bloomed in gardens everywhere. A feeling of "newness" filled the air.

After church on Easter Sunday, Mandie and Celia sat at the dinner table with Mrs. Taft and Hilda, the dark-haired, disturbed girl whom Mrs. Taft had given a home. Hilda still couldn't talk much, and Mrs. Taft had told Mandie that the girl still ran away occasionally when she got a chance. But Hilda was excited to see Mandie. That made Mandie feel good after all the rough treatment she had gotten from the girls at school lately.

Now, as the others ate and talked, Hilda sat quietly and listened.

"Amanda, dear," Mrs. Taft said as Ella, the maid, refilled her coffee cup, "we need to begin planning our trip to Europe, you know." She smiled and turned to Celia. "And Celia, I have obtained permission from your mother for you to go, too."

The girls began to talk excitedly.

"Also," Mrs. Taft raised her voice to get their attention, "It seems that Senator Morton will be sailing on the same ship that we'll take. Isn't that nice?"

Mandie and Celia looked at each other and giggled. Mandie had told her friend about the senator.

"That's great, Grandmother," Mandie agreed. Then she realized that she had not heard a word from her mother about the proposed trip to Europe. "But did you ever ask *my* mother if I could go?" she asked.

"Of course, dear," Mrs. Taft replied, cutting a slice of ham. "Your mother and I got that settled long ago—in fact, right after we came back from Washington. I'm sorry if I didn't remember to tell you."

"Thanks, Grandmother." Mandie jumped up and ran around the table to give her a hug. "I love you. You're a wonderful grandmother."

Hilda's big brown eyes sparkled. "Love you," she said.

Everyone smiled at the girl's recognition of the words.

"Well, Amanda," Mrs. Taft said, "I don't know what brought that on, but sit back down now, dear, and let's get our plans made."

There was a lot of discussion about where to go, what to see, and what they would need to take with them. Mandie was excited that Celia would be able to go with them this time. "When are we going?" she asked.

"I've thought about that," Mrs. Taft replied. "And your mother and I agreed that we should wait until after your little sister or brother is born in June, so I have made reservations to spend the whole month of July in Europe.

"We have to wait that long?" Mandie said, disappointed.

"Well, we can't go before the baby comes, and your

mother may want me around for awhile afterward, so July is about the soonest we could go."

Mandie grumbled to herself. That baby was causing trouble again, even before it got here. She would be glad when it finally came. Then maybe it would quit interfering with her plans.

After the meal, Mandie went to the kitchen to feed Snowball, who had patiently waited at her feet under the table. As Mandie entered the kitchen, she saw Ben sitting at the table having his dinner.

She flashed a quick smile. "I just want to give this cat something to eat," she said, stooping to put some food scraps onto a plate on the floor. "You look all tired out, Ben. Where've you been this morning?"

"Out to de farm," Ben replied without thinking. Then he clasped his hand over his mouth, and his eyes grew wide.

Mandie looked up. "The farm where they grow the vegetables for our food at school?" she asked, hoping now she might find out what had been going on out there. She tried not to sound too eager. "I remember one time Aunt Phoebe took me out there," she said innocently. "I met Uncle Cal's mother, Aunt Pansy—she really runs the place, doesn't she? And her son Willie and granddaughter Soony help, too, right?"

"Yessum, they does all right, Missy," Ben agreed. "But I thinks I done said too much already."

"Oh, come on, Ben," Mandie pleaded. "You can tell me. My curiosity is killing me."

"My, my, my," Ben replied.

Mandie could tell he was giving in.

"I s'pose it be all over now, so it don't matter so much nohow." Ben wiped his mouth with the back of his hand.

"Well, it be like dis, Missy," he began. "Dat Willie, he be out in de field somewheres and dat Soony, she be gone somewheres else. And Miz Pansy, she be all alone in de house."

Mandie felt shivers up and down her spine, not knowing what to expect.

"And you know Miz Pansy, she always be good to po' folks to try an' he'p 'em," he continued. "So when dis young Negro fellow come knockin' at de back do' and ask fo' food, she lets him in de kitchen and sets a plate of hot dumplin's b'fo' him." Ben stopped and took a drink of coffee.

Mandie's heartbeat quickened. "Please hurry, Ben," she urged. "Tell me what happened!"

"Well, dat fellow, he be up to no good. He tie up Miz Pansy after he beat her down when she wouldn't give in to be tied up. Den he rob de whole house," Ben explained. "He took—"

"Ben," Mandie interrupted, "is Aunt Pansy all right? Why did Miss Prudence keep all this a secret?"

"Miz Pansy, she done be recovered now," Ben said with a mouthful of biscuit. "And dat Miz Prudence, she be a funny person. She don't want nobody to tell 'cause it might hurt de school, she say. Ain't dat funny?"

"Oh, I wish Miss Prudence had let us know so we could have gone to visit Aunt Pansy," Mandie said. "I suppose since she's Uncle Cal's mother, that's why he and Aunt Phoebe were disappearing now and then. I'm going to ask if I can visit Aunt Pansy."

"Now don't you be tellin' dat Miz Prudence dat you knows 'bout dis," Ben warned, 'cause she know den dat I told you."

"How would she know *you* told me?" Mandie asked.

"Because I was de one what took Miz Hope and Aunt Phoebe out dere," Ben explained.

"Then Grandmother must have known about it," Mandie said, confused.

"No, all dis happen when yo' grandmother ain't home," Ben replied. "And Miz Prudence, she say don't tell nobody, so I don't tell nobody." He shook his head vigorously. "Till now," he added sheepishly.

Mandie put her hands on her hips, exasperated at Miss Prudence's secrecy. "I'll just ask if I can go visit Aunt Pansy," Mandie said. "I won't mention anything about the robbery or her being hurt."

Mandie didn't mention the matter to her grandmother either, but as soon as they arrived back at the school later that day, Mandie told Celia what had happened, and they made plans to visit Aunt Pansy.

One Saturday soon afterward, Mandie and Celia were allowed to visit the old woman when Aunt Phoebe had to go out to the farm for supplies. Aunt Pansy was delighted to see the girls, and no one mentioned the robbery. Everything seemed to be back to normal.

---

Later that month, while Mandie and Celia sat on the window seat in their room, enjoying the warm night breeze that floated in through the open window, Mandie was brooding about the way the other girls were still treating her. Suddenly she heard a faint noise below. She leaned forward to look down into the yard. "Did you hear something?"

"I think so," Celia replied, glancing out into the night. "It sounded like a bird."

Mandie peered outside, surveying the entire lawn below. The full moon illuminated the school grounds fairly well except for the shadows from the huge magnolia trees. A figure stepped out of the shadows. Mandie caught her breath. "Look, Celia! It's Uncle Ned!" she cried excitedly. "I'm going down there a minute."

"Mandie, please don't get caught," Celia warned. "The curfew bell hasn't rung yet, and there may be other people around."

"I'll be right back," Mandie promised.

Racing down the servants' stairs and through the deserted kitchen, she ran out into the yard. "Uncle Ned!" she exclaimed, giving him a hug.

The old Indian pointed to a bench in the shadow of the tree, and she sat down next to him. "How is school?" he asked.

"Not wonderful," Mandie replied. "It's been weeks since I got back from Washington, and the other girls still won't speak to me." Her blue eyes quickly filled with tears. "I hear them making remarks behind my back. They say I'm stuck up since I met the President, and they say, 'Who does she think she is?' and things like that."

Uncle Ned cupped his hand under her chin and looked at her closely. "Is Papoose stuck up?" he asked.

"Why, no," she responded quickly. Then pausing for a moment, she added, "I don't think I am. At least I don't mean to be. Oh, I don't know what's going on."

"Maybe Papoose cause all this bad feeling," the old Indian suggested. "Maybe other girls jealous because Papoose get special treatment."

Mandie sat there quietly for a minute, looking deep into his dark eyes. "I think they are jealous, but what can I do about it?" she asked.

"Could be Papoose brag too much. Think self too

important," Uncle Ned suggested. "Remember how grandmother of Papoose act with school head lady about Papoose not going to Washington? Papoose not like. Grandmother of Papoose act too important."

"Oh, Uncle Ned, maybe I have been thinking I was pretty great after all the things that I was able to see and do in Washington," Mandie admitted reluctantly. "But if I have been bragging, I haven't meant to."

"Other girls not know this," Uncle Ned replied. "Remember, Papoose also got special leave from school. Other girls not get these things."

"What should I do, Uncle Ned?" Mandie asked, hanging her head.

"Papoose must be friendly with other girls, stop talk about trip to Washington, tell girls sorry you brag," the old Indian replied.

Mandie looked up quickly. "But, Uncle Ned, I couldn't apologize to them," she protested. "They caused it all!"

"Not matter who caused," Uncle Ned explained. "Remember Big Book say pride go before fall. Must make girls understand you their friend."

"All right, Uncle Ned," Mandie agreed. "I'll try. I've really been miserable. Celia is the only friend I have left."

"Not true," Uncle Ned objected. "I friend of Papoose." He smiled.

Mandie reached up and gave him a big hug. "Thanks, Uncle Ned. But now I'd better get back upstairs," she said, looking around.

"Wait, Papoose. I not finished," said the old Indian. "I bring message from mother of Papoose. She say tell Papoose that *new* papoose arrive."

"Mother's baby has been born?" Mandie could hardly believe her ears. "It's not time yet."

"New Papoose come early, but it fine," Uncle Ned explained.

Mandie was surprised to find herself getting excited. "Is it a boy or girl?" she asked.

"I not know, Papoose," the Indian replied.

"You mean my mother didn't tell you?"

"No, not tell. Mother of Papoose say she want to tell Papoose when Papoose come home from school," he explained.

"When was it born, Uncle Ned?" Mandie asked, frustrated at not knowing whether she had a brother or a sister.

"On full moon, Sunday the twenty-first day of April this month," the old Indian replied. He stood up, towering over Mandie. "Must go now. Remember, be nice to other girls, like we talk, Papoose."

"I'll try, Uncle Ned," Mandie promised. "I'll try real hard." She stood and squeezed his hand. "And tell my mother that as far as I know right now, I'll be out of school the last week of May."

"I tell mother of Papoose," he promised. "Big God bless Papoose." He stooped briefly and kissed Mandie on the forehead before disappearing into the shadows.

Mandie slowly made her way back into the house and up the stairs to her room. Why didn't her mother let her know whether the baby was a boy or girl? Now she would have to wait a whole month before she could find out.

Although she felt a touch of anger and jealousy over the thought of sharing her mother, she also realized that she was actually excited about finally seeing the baby.

# Cooking with Mandie!

Mandie
Apron & Bonnet
Pattern Included in
Mandie's Cookbook

After days and days of begging, Mandie finally convinced Aunt Lou to teach her how to cook. You know who Aunt Lou is—Mandie's Uncle John's Housekeeper. Mandie not only loved learning how to cook, but she recorded every recipe, every "do" and "don't" that they went through. And that is how this cookbook came to be.

Mandie also learned how to cook Cherokee-style from Morning Star, Uncle Ned's wife. Sallie, her granddaughter, helped translate since Morning Star doesn't speak English. Being part Cherokee, Mandie wanted to learn how her kin-people cook.

With Mandie's step-by-step instructions, you can cook and serve meals and share the experiences of girls from the turn of the century. Learn how to bake cakes and pies, do popcorn balls, make biscuits and Southern fried chicken, as well as make Indian recipes like dried apples and potato skins.

***If you love the Mandie Books,***
***you'll love to try cooking***
***Mandie's favorite recipes!***